90

It's Me, Jennifer

by Jane Sorenson

D1540315

STANDARD PUBLISHING
Cincinnati, Ohio   2931

Library of Congress Cataloging in Publication Data

Sorenson, Jane.
    It's me, Jennifer.

    Summary: Jennifer and her two brothers are sent to Sunday
school for the first time after one of her brothers takes the Lord's
name in vain.
    [1. Christian life—Fiction]   I. Title.
PZ7.S7214It   1984   [Fic]   84-217
ISBN 0-87239-771-8

To Steve
    encourager, friend, son . . .
    and the one who found a home for Jennifer

1

I Introduce Myself

Lord, I guess it's about time we met. My name is Jennifer Andrews Green. But You can call me Jennifer if You want to.

I don't think we've ever met before, but maybe You've seen me around. I'm the girl with the long, straight brown hair, medium height and weight. That describes some other girls, too, but I'm the one with the big mouth. You know, the one who's always talking.

And Lord, You probably already know it, but yesterday was my first day in Sunday school. I guess You must hang around churches a lot.

Well, anyway, the real reason I went was because I had no choice. My parents decided last Tuesday that it was the right time for me and my two brothers to start Sunday school. My brothers are Peter Green and Justin Green, and if You were there yesterday, You already know that they are what Mom calls active.

I don't want You to think we're not religious. We take turns saying a prayer every night at dinner. Unless, of course, we're having something quick, like pancakes or pizza. And we always pray when Grandma and Grandpa Green are with us. They even pray in restaurants!

Well, as usual, I got off the point. Tuesday night was the last straw. Pete talked back to Mom, and when she sent him to his room, he said, "Oh, God!" And he wasn't praying, I could tell. Swearing is against the rules in our house. We are big on *respect*.

I won't go into details, but we were all told to be dressed up (no jeans) and ready to go at 9:15 Sunday morning. Mom would be driving us to church. And Dad would be having his "day of rest." I think that meant he could sleep in and then read the newspaper while we were gone.

Mom got up and fixed our breakfast and made sure the boys' shirts were tucked in. I wore my best skirt and pink sweater. We really looked nice. At least I thought so. I hope You noticed.

Mom dropped us off and told me to get Pete and Justin to the right classes. Just how I was going to do that, plus find my own class, I had no idea.

But lucky for me, there was a nice man at the door who seemed to have things under control. He sent the boys quickly with women who seemed to know the ropes. Just as he got to me, I saw my friend Laurie.

"Hi," she said. "What are you doing here?"

"The same thing you are," I answered. "I'm going to find out all about God. This *is* the right place, isn't it?"

"Oh, sure," Laurie said, smiling. "I was just surprised to see you. Come on with me, and I'll show you where our class is."

I walked with her down the hall, which was so filled with kids that I didn't see You anywhere.

"First we have opening exercises," Laurie whispered as we entered a large room. I was surprised, because I never realized You had a physical fitness program. Since the girls were on one side and the boys on the other, I was kind of worried because all the girls were wearing skirts.

Well, that's how dumb I was about Sunday school. We didn't do any exercises at all—unless you call standing up and singing exercise, which personally I don't. Altogether we sang three songs, one sitting down, two standing up. I had never heard any of them before.

Then the man in charge asked us to bow our heads for prayer, so naturally I did. All of a sudden his voice sounded so strange that I wondered if it was really the same man, so I peeked. It was. I kept my eyes closed from then on in case somebody else peeked.

At the end, the leader told us to join him in praying the Lord's Prayer. I think I was the only one who didn't know the words. Naturally I didn't want to look stupid, so I faked it by moving my lips *respectfully*. I knew we were praying to You, but everybody went so fast that I couldn't catch most of it. Is Your name Hallowed B.?

Well, next we went into little areas curtained off from each other. The boys were acting immature, just like in school. The girls were pretending not to notice.

Our class had five girls, counting me. And we had our own teacher, Miss Gregg. She is young, as teachers go, but she seems to know a lot about You. Mostly I noticed that she was interested in the girls. She asked Laurie how her grandma was, (much better) and if we had something called "prayer requests." Nobody said anything, so I guess we didn't have them.

The lesson was about a blind man. Jesus mixed spit and mud and put it on the man's eyes. It seemed pretty gross to me, but it did the trick. When the blind man washed it off, he could see. The teacher said that was a miracle. I agree!

When the time was up, I was anxious to find my brothers, 'cause there's no telling what they might've been up to. But first I decided to ask Miss Gregg about something that was bothering me.

"Is God's name really Hallowed B?" I asked.

It took Miss Gregg by surprise, I could tell. Then she looked as if she might laugh, but I guess she didn't want to make me feel stupid.

"Not really," she said. "Praying is just talking to God. You can tell Him anything at all any time you want to."

"But what is His name?" I asked.

"You can just begin by saying, Dear Lord," she said.

Then Miss Gregg smiled and put her arm around my shoulder. It was the first time a teacher ever did that to me. I kinda liked it.

Well, suddenly I remembered Pete and Justin, so I had to get going fast. Luckily they were punching each other out, not someone else. I gave them as good an imitation of Mom's *look* as I could. They stopped and followed me out the door.

You know, Lord, I think we could be good friends. I've always wanted to know about You. Did You see me at Sunday school? I hope so, 'cause I was there.

2

High School Game

Dear Lord, it's me, Jennifer.

Tonight was so important that I just have to tell somebody about it. I sure hope You aren't bored by basketball.

Maybe You're wondering why I've suddenly started telling You about my life. Well, there are several reasons.

Mom and Dad are good parents, as parents go. She's a room mother at school, and he's something called a sales engineer. On a scale of one to ten in the strictness department, they are about elevens. But deep down, I'll have to admit that they really care about me. Which is more than I can say about some parents I've observed.

Anyhow, I do talk a lot. And sometimes they listen.

But there are some things a girl just can't tell her parents. Maybe if I had an older brother or sister that would do the trick, but in my case I'm the oldest. That means I have to go through everything first with no experience.

I do have friends. But my "best friend" can change from one week to the next, which means that my secrets may suddenly be known by a blabbermouth who tells all! And even the secrets themselves change quite often. For instance, my goals in life, the teacher I like best, or which boy (if any) has talked to me.

Last year I tried keeping a diary, but that had its own problems. On the boring days, there wasn't anything special to write about. And on the special days, there weren't enough lines in the book, plus I wouldn't have time to write anyway.

I have noticed that when Grandma and Grandpa Green pray, they just talk to You naturally. What I mean is, they don't memorize what they say. They sound just the same as when they're talking to anyone else, which is why I've decided to tell You stuff, too.

Well, back to basketball. Today was the best day of my life so far. Two of my friends invited me to go to the high-school tournament game. Being the oldest, I always have to do things first. I'm sure by the time Justin is my age, he'll just say, "I'm going to the game tonight with Todd," and Mom will say "OK."

In my case, everything is a big deal. When Susan called to invite me, I had to call her back because it took my family so long to discuss it. *Who was going? What time would we be home? How come we wanted to go to a high-school game when we never stayed for those at our own school? Whose brother was driving?* Well, I'd just about given up hope that I'd ever get to do anything but watch TV on a Friday night when my parents said yes!

I was so excited I could hardly eat my spaghetti. And I cleared the table before my father finished his coffee. I had so much time to get dressed that I tried on three different outfits and still couldn't decide what to wear.

Susan's brother, Mark, was the driver, and he didn't seem too thrilled at having us ride along. But Susan said her dad told him that since he could drive, taking his sister places went with the territory. I didn't really understand what he meant, but it was a lot more fun than riding with a parent. We picked up Laurie on the way. But once we got to the high school, Mark pretended he didn't know us anyway.

The gym seemed huge compared to our baby one. At first Susan, Laurie, and I sat down in the bleachers and watched the teams practice. We were for the orange shirts. I'd never seen so many tall boys! And not just the players, either. Almost every guy in the building was taller than Gretchen Soney, which is quite a contrast from junior high.

By the time the game started, Susan suggested we go to the refreshment stand. As we walked slowly around the gym, I sure was glad I'd worn my pink sweater. It was perfect. The teams ran back and forth, and the crowd cheered and groaned. I looked up at the scoreboard, and we were winning 10 to 6. We kept on walking even when some boys told us to sit down.

Once we were so close to a cheerleader I could have touched her. Of course, I really wouldn't have, but that's how close. She swung her pleated skirt, waved her arms, and smiled like she'd just won a million-dollars-for-life contest. I decided then and there that law school could very well wait. I would concentrate on becoming a cheerleader!

I'll bet we walked ten miles tonight, up and down that big gym. I'm not really sure why either. But Susan knows about things like that, and I'll just have to fake it until I get it figured out.

You'll be glad to hear I got home on time. So were Mom and Dad! I think Mark was really in a hurry to take us home, but Laurie and I were so excited we didn't mind.

My dad wanted to know if we won, and I told him we did. But before he could ask the score, I was already here in my room.

3

My Birthday

Dear Lord, it's me, Jennifer.

Mom has never enjoyed slumber parties. I mean, having them or us kids going to them. For a long time she wouldn't let me go to any because I needed my sleep. And I couldn't have one because she and Dad needed their sleep.

Finally persuaded that my social life would end before it ever began, she gave in. But only because it was my birthday. Is my guess right that Dad was on my side? He often sees the fun in something.

Well, the point is that last week I got to ask five girls, including my cousin. So it wasn't a very big slumber party, but the truth is I only have four best friends now anyhow. All of them could come: Beth, Susan, Laurie, Linda, and my cousin Sarah.

Actually, Sarah goes to another school, but my other friends have all met her. Have You? Her family goes to Calvary Church, if that helps. They are also named Green—Robert and Carol, Sarah and Michael.

Well, when Friday night finally came, the girls all said hi to my parents on the way in. Mom and Dad were playing a game at the kitchen table with Aunt Mary and Uncle Dick. Then my friends carried their sleeping bags and birthday gifts downstairs to our rec room.

"What would you like to do?" I asked. Everybody was quiet. Nobody said a word. Just silence. I felt DOOM. The party was a flop.

"Oh, anything," Beth finally said. By then I had forgotten my question! I found myself almost wishing Mom were there directing games like she used to do at my parties.

"Want to play Ping-Pong?" I hoped I didn't sound desperate.

"Sure!" But then we realized there were six of us.

"How about some round-robin Ping-Pong?" I tried again.

"Great," said Linda.

Well, as we got into the swing of things, I felt better. It was going to be fun after all.

Nobody was all that good at playing the game of Ping-Pong, which really made it more fun. (In other words, there was no competition!) So we just made mistakes, laughed, and got so sweaty that we had to sit down to have Pepsis.

"Hey, Birthday Girl," said Sarah, "how about opening your presents?"

"I can hardly wait," I laughed. "I thought you'd never get tired of Ping-Pong."

"Oh, ho," said Susan. "Just for that we'll make you wait!"

But by then I was tearing into the first package, a small square box. "Wow! A pearl ring. Where's the card?"

"It's from me," Sarah said. "To tell you the truth, it's from our whole family. Happy birthday, cousin!"

"Lucky you," said Beth. "I wish I had cousins nearby!"

"Thanks a lot, Sarah! And tell Michael and your folks thanks, too."

"Glad you like it. Does it fit?"

I slipped it on my third finger. "Perfect!"

"Wrong hand, Jennifer," said Susan. "Save that one for your engagement ring. This one goes on your right hand."

I changed the ring, feeling dumb. But I grinned anyway. "Perfect on this hand, too," I said.

The birthday card pictured a beautiful sunset over a lake. It said in gold, "May God Keep You in His Care on Your Birthday and Always." I don't know how they found out I'm going to Sunday school. Anyway, I decided to read the card later in my room. I hope that didn't hurt Your feelings!

The next gift was from Beth. It had a nice card about being friends a long time. She gave me a long T-shirt printed with my name and a rainbow.

"Mom helped pick it out," Beth said. "Hope you like it."

"Like it? It's great!" We smiled at each other. We have been friends a long time.

Susan, who knows how much I like to read, brought me a set of mysteries. I opened the first one.

"Oh, no you don't," laughed Susan. "It's your party, and we want to have fun with you. Save them for a dateless evening." Everybody laughed. None of our parents would let us go out with a boy even if we asked. And no one has.

"Very funny," I added. "Hey, thanks a million!"

"You're welcome a million," Susan said. "Can I read them later?"

The next box was flat, and the card was a funny Snoopy one from Linda. Inside the thin white paper was something made of white terrycloth. I pulled it out and held it up. "Wow! A swimsuit cover-up!"

Everyone squealed their appreciation. Linda looked sort of embarrassed. "My mom made it for you," she said. "She sews a lot."

"It's perfect!" I screamed. "Now all I need is a bathing suit."

"Are you getting a new one?" somebody asked.

"Are you kidding! Or maybe you don't remember mine from last year!"

"Two-piece?" Beth asked.

"Dad finally said I can," I grinned.

"Yeahhhhhhh!" everyone cheered.

"One more box to go," I said. "Must be from Laurie."

"Whatever makes you think that?" she laughed.

It was a little bottle of Charlie spray cologne—my favorite. But the card was different. It wasn't funny, and it wasn't gushy. I read it silently. "Hey, guys," I said, "I want you to hear this card." They listened as I read. It said that life is like a gift full of wonder and surprises, all tied up with a ribbon of dreams.

When I finished, it was as quiet as it had been at the beginning of the party, but altogether different. Nobody felt embarrassed. I think the word is awed. Am I right, Lord?

Mom broke the silence by opening the door at the top of the stairway.

"Pizza time," she called.

We all had different ideas about what to order. "Just please, no onions!" "Is the sausage hot?" "But I love mushrooms!" Finally we decided, and Dad left to pick up our special orders of pizza.

"Only one thing missing," said Susan.

"What's that?" I asked.

"Boys!"

"Boys? You have a one-track mind!"

"When we're older," Susan explained, "the boys will find out about our overnights and pretend they're trying to get in!" Her brother, Mark, must have told her. I hoped Mom hadn't heard that boys sometimes do things like that.

"Well, that's probably part of the 'wonder and surprises' on that last card," I suggested.

"Sounds good to me."

Everyone was talking and laughing and drinking Pepsi and eating pizza and I knew my birthday party was a success.

Later on, the kitchen door opened. "All right, down there," Dad said, using his stern voice. "That's it. Quiet now!"

After the lights were out, somebody whispered. "Just think, boys!"

"Maybe next year."

And then the room was quiet for the third and last time.

4

My First Two-Piece Suit

Lord, it's me, Jennifer.

I really don't know who dreaded today most, Mom or me.

In my head I see visions of a girl running on the beach, or getting golden brown on a colorful towel, or diving into a pool. Always she's smiling.

But behind every such picture looms the bathing-suit purchase. When I was younger, it was no problem. Mom would find my size and either ask if I wanted the blue one ("You always look nice in blue, Dear") or the pink cotton print. It was already understood that a two piece was a no-no (forbidden by camp regulations) and that white "made you look like you had nothing on when it got wet."

Besides white was certain to end up the season a greenish gray, the ugliest color imaginable.

And, anyway, I didn't really care too much when I was younger what anyone thought. The kids back then who were "out of it" at the pool were those scared to put their faces in the water. They thought that even a nose-holding jump from the low dive was OK for a while.

But now that boys have started noticing us (and vice versa), nobody even cares if you get wet! The big thing is to make a good impression. Translated, that means that how you look in a bathing suit rates twice as much as a decent backstroke.

I suspect that for girls like Amanda Lynn Daniels bathing suits will never be a problem of any kind. One year pink cotton print, the next year movie star perfection! And real swimmers like Karen Bush—those who train at the Y all winter—just buy another tank suit and wonder why the rest of us have such a hard time.

Well, back to the point. I will remind You that Dad finally gave me permission to get a two-piece suit—on the condition that he approved of it. Anyhow, Mom picked me up at school and we headed for the shopping mall. I was hoping nobody would see me there with her! She kept acting cheerful but I could tell she felt DOOM.

We started at the department store where we have a charge account. When the sales girl approached, Mom clearly took control. "We'd like to see bathing suits for my daughter," she said firmly.

"What size?" the sales girl asked.

I thought it was a reasonable request, but right away Mom lost her cool.

"I'm not quite sure," she said. "Why don't you give us several two-piece suits for her to try on?"

Not a word this year about color, I noticed. Obviously, to both of us, the big thing was going to be how it fit.

With three suits (the most permitted, even for girls with their mothers) we headed for the dressing rooms.

"I don't want you to come in," I told Mom. We both realized this wasn't going to be easy.

"All right, Jennifer," Mom said. "But I could help you fasten things."

"If I need help, I'll ask," I said.

Pulling the curtain shut, I could see that my mother already looked tired.

I stripped to my underpants and pulled on the yellow bottom. Perfect fit! I could hardly believe my good luck. But, You guessed it, the top was another story. I managed to get it on by fastening the hook first, turning it around, and slipping my arms through the straps. There it hung.

"How are you doing?" Mom asked through the curtain in a weak, high voice.

"Not so good," I admitted.

"May I come in?" she asked.

"I guess so," I answered.

I felt embarrassed that anyone, even Mom, should see me.

"Well," was all Mom could say. Then she handed me the aqua suit. "Why not try another one? Nobody settles for the very first one anyway." Her attempted cheerful-ness made me feel a little better.

"This one has more elastic," she pointed out. "It should be better. May I stay?"

"Absolutely not!"

So she went back into the hall.

"Hey, Mom," I almost shouted. "I think this is it!"

Mom popped through the curtain before I could stop her. Oh, well, I was so excited I didn't even care. But I did refuse to look at her as I pulled up the aqua bottom.

I should say as I *tried* to pull up the aqua bottom. It looked like it would fit a kindergartner, and the elastic didn't stretch enough for me to get it over my hips. I really couldn't believe it. I don't even *have* hips!

"I don't know why manufacturers can't manage to make bathing suits that have the same size top and bottom," Mom said softly.

"Maybe it's just that I don't have the same size top and bottom," I suggested.

"Nonsense," said Mom. "Even grown women have the same problem." She paused. "Would you consider a one piece?"

"Never," I whispered.

"Well then, how about this blue one?"

"Please leave," I said. I thought I might start crying any minute.

Mom went.

I couldn't decide whether to begin with the bottom or the top. It really didn't seem to matter, so I pulled on the bottom. It felt fine. Then I hooked the top, switched it around, and put the straps over my shoulders. One look and I started laughing like crazy.

"What's so funny, Jennifer?" Mom wondered. "May I come in?"

When I didn't answer, because I was laughing so hard, she came in. One look and she started laughing, too. It must have been catching, because suddenly we could hear people in the other little dressing rooms joining us.

"Mom," I gasped. "Did you ever imagine me looking like this?"

"Can't say that I ever did," she answered, with tears running down her cheeks. "It must be the way the cups are sewn in."

"It isn't me, that's for sure," I said, quieting down for a second, only to be overcome once more by another wave of laughter.

Well, there's nothing like a good laugh to clear the air. And once I started enjoying myself, the afternoon took a turn for the better.

Not that we lucked out right away. It was, in fact, five stores later when we settled on a black suit with a top that fit and pants that were too big. Mom was sure that she could take them in with a few small tucks that wouldn't show.

"What if Dad thinks black is too grown-up?" I asked Mom on the way home.

"This is one time," she answered firmly, "when I couldn't care less."

5

Love Match

Lord, it's me, Jennifer.

Can a person help it if she's competitive? What I mean is, whenever I play games, I like to win. Even when I pretend I don't care (which is one way to get people to like you more), I still know, deep down inside, that I'd hate to lose.

Now, it's easier to understand if there's a prize. At the fair I've seen high-school guys throw balls trying their best to knock down some pins. And I can't imagine what they'd ever do with a stuffed animal.

Me, I want to win even if there isn't a prize! And that's what ruined my life Saturday.

To begin at the beginning, Beth and I didn't have anything to do. And it was too nice a day to do nothing. So we decided to play tennis at the park. Luck was on our side. The center court was empty. We didn't even care that it was the one with the saggy net.

At first we just volleyed. That means hitting the ball back and forth without following the rules or keeping score. It was fun just to be playing. But gradually I realized that my backhand had really improved. I mean 100 percent! And now, all of a sudden, I was feeling like a new teenage pro.

Not only had my backhand improved, but usually when I returned the ball I could make it land on Beth's backhand side. And her backhand hadn't improved. That is probably why she didn't act too thrilled when I suggested we start to keep score.

Did You know that the tennis pros seem to think that serving is a special treat? Probably that's because they're good at it. In our case, serving is usually a handicap. But, because Beth wasn't acting too pleased about playing real games, I offered to begin serving. She seemed to cheer up a little.

I blew my first two chances. That meant I was already losing love-thirty, and we hadn't even hit the ball back and forth once yet. So I really concentrated on my next serve. It wasn't exactly an ace, but at least we were playing. Thanks to my backhand (and Beth's), I won the next point. In fact, I won the first game.

"Your serve," I said.

Because Beth's serves are better than mine, she took

the second game. And that's when I really started feeling competitive. I was trying so hard to win that I didn't even notice that Todd and Jeff had started playing on the left-hand court when the other couple left.

My serve became stronger, and I could picture myself playing in a big tournament. Maybe even Wimbledon.

Beth must have been thinking about Todd, because her game fell apart totally. At the end of the set, I was the winner. And Todd was asking Beth if he could walk her home.

Well, that left Jeff and me alone together. I felt strange, especially since I had never said a word to him. Luckily, he spoke first. "Good set," he said.

"Thanks," I answered. I'd seen him at band practice, but I didn't want to bring that up.

"How about playing with me," Jeff suggested.

Lord, when a boy asks you to play tennis, is that a date? I felt excited and shy all at the same time. But I knew I had to say something. I finally said, "OK."

I soon discovered that Jeff's backhand wasn't all that great either, but I figured he'd cream me anyhow. We began to relax the longer we volleyed. It was fun. And I, Jennifer, was playing tennis with a boy!

He said he'd serve first if I wanted to play him a set. That was fine with me. But the first ball skimmed over the net, bounced in the corner, and sailed past me before I could even get a good grip on my racket. That's when I learned what it felt like to be "aced." Of course, Jeff won the first game.

Well, you guessed it. I started feeling competitive again. I concentrated on every ball. I forgot about everything except tennis. All I wanted to do was win.

I will say it was pretty close. But Jeff obviously wasn't thrilled to lose either. "Got to go now," he said. "See ya."

When I got home Mom was in the kitchen. I was glad because I really wanted to talk to someone. "I'm getting pretty good at tennis," I said. "I beat Beth and even a boy."

"When I was your age, a girl was never supposed to beat a boy," Mom said. "It hurts their egos."

"Things are different now, Mom," I said. "Girls can do anything boys can do."

"I know," Mom said. She shook salt on the chicken. I kept waiting for her to say something else. She didn't.

So here I am, Lord. At least in tennis you know the rules. Isn't a girl supposed to do her best? Is it wrong to want to win? What am I supposed to do about it? And how come I feel like the biggest loser of all?

6

Independence Day

Lord, it's me, Jennifer.

The Fourth of July is big in our town. At least that's what everybody here thinks.

Going to the parade is *traditional*. Our family sits with the Archers in their yard on lawn chairs. They live on Main Street. Personally, I think it's sort of a cheap way to get a good spot.

Well, anyway the parade is not the Rose Bowl, but we do have floats, a queen, bands, and fire engines at the end. Last year there were two groups on horseback. I thought they were the best.

Sometimes my brothers have decorated their bikes for the parade. Once Pete won first place. Dad helped him.

Justin does his own, and he never wins anything. But he keeps trying, I'll say that for him.

Anyhow, this year was special because I got to ride on a float. Our scout group acted out Betsy Ross sewing the flag. I was not Betsy Ross, but I got to hold the corner while Beth pretended to sew.

It was fun waving to everybody from the float, even though I didn't know them. I felt kind of like a princess. My costume was colonial. But the white wig was hot and my head was sweaty underneath. As we reached the Archers' yard, my family and all the Archers clapped and cheered—especially my dad. I could have died, so I pretended not to know them and looked the other way.

"I love a parade," sang my father at the top of his lungs when we got home. "Best one yet," he said when we all got together for our picnic. "And next year Jennifer will be queen. And Pete and Justin can wear their Little League uniforms and bat bubble gum into the crowd." Pete and I groaned.

"I'm not old enough to be queen," I said. "Even if I were pretty enough, which I certainly am not."

"Nonsense," said Dad. "How old do you have to be?"

"I don't know," I said. "Just older. Maybe I could ride a horse."

"Sure," said Pete. "And I'll ride a Harley-Davidson! And forget that Little League stuff, Dad. I'm not going out for it."

Justin watched with interest. "I think batting bubble gum at the crowd would be fun! Could I keep some?"

30

The Fourth of July is a *tradition,* always the same. Grandma and Grandpa Andrews always come. Plus the aunts and uncles and cousins that live in town. It's always at our house, 'cause we have a big yard.

Uncle Bob and Aunt Carol were really excited because the float for Green's Furniture Store had won a red ribbon. The banner said, "Home Is Where the Heart Is," and the float carried a playhouse. Our cousins, Sarah and Michael, rode on the float.

"Wasn't it fun?" I whispered to Sarah. "I mean riding and waving to everyone?"

"Shhhh," whispered Sarah. "John smiled at me and waved!"

"No! You lucky duck. Did anyone see?"

"Course not, Jennifer. Dad would kill me!"

"I know," I said. Our fathers are a lot alike, being brothers and all.

"Here come Matt and Joshua," Justin yelled. They are the Andrews cousins who are his heroes 'cause they're in high school sports. Sarah and I think they are very handsome. Also, they're the only older boys we know. Uncle Dick and Aunt Mary came too. She brought her special German potato salad.

It was our good old *traditional* Fourth of July. The food's the same every year, which is fine with me.

After we ate, Matthew and Joshua excused themselves and left. Mom went in the house for insect repellent and our blankets. "Almost time for the fireworks," she reminded.

"Do we have to go?" Sarah asked.

I thought maybe a bolt of lightning would strike her dead! I looked at Uncle Bob first, then at Dad.

"We always go to the fireworks," said Uncle Bob. And Dad nodded in agreement.

Sarah didn't know enough to quit. She added, "But it's so boring! And I hate the mosquitoes."

At that point Mom came out carrying a tiny green bottle. "Behold," she said, "something new. It's guaranteed to repel mosquitoes, black flies, gnats, chiggers, ticks, and fleas for three hours."

"Sounds like that should take care of it," said Dad. "Everyone get a lawn chair or blanket." They ignored Sarah.

We parked as close as we could, then walked the rest of the way to the park. Personally, I had never realized just how boring fireworks are. Bang! Bang! Squeal of voices, followed by "Ahhhhhhhhhhhhh!" over and over again. Sure, different colors and shapes, but there's only so many things you can do with colored lights!

Sarah and I sat together. I tried to look just as bored as she was trying to look. We couldn't talk because we'd get dirty looks. Finally the dusk turned to darkness.

Suddenly I felt a light touch on my arm. At first I thought the insect stuff had failed. But then I looked around. There, on the edge of the next blanket was Eric Swenson! When the fireworks exploded into a huge green umbrella, I could see his blond hair. Then it was dark again.

Sarah suddenly looked up at the sky as if she could hardly wait for the next fireworks display.

"Hi!" Eric whispered. "Can't stay. Family's here."

I nodded. I understood.

"You were beautiful on the float," Eric whispered. Boom. Boom. Squeal. "Ahhhhhhhhhhhhh." He was gone.

I whispered to Sarah, "First time he's ever spoken to me."

"Wow," Sarah whispered back.

The family started looking at us. We settled back and silently looked at the sky.

Boom. Boom, boom, BOOM! BOOM! The whole air was filled with lights. It was the finale. Sarah and I both smiled and joined the others when they said, "Ahhhhhhhhhhhhhhh!"

7

Oral Surgery

Lord, it's me, Jennifer.

It really is too bad dentists have such a bad reputation. I wonder if they have any friends at all? I mean besides You.

I got the first of my braces on right after school was out. It seemed just like another part of growing up. Don't You ever do a perfect job on teeth anymore? Mom said when she was a girl she was the only one in junior high with braces. She felt very self-conscious, which must have been awful. Now nearly everybody's got an orthodontist.

However, I think this oral surgery is too much! As You know, I've been dreading it for weeks. I asked You to help me, and I shudder to think what it would have been like if You hadn't!

I woke up early yesterday with a stomachache and a feeling of DOOM. Thanks for taking away the stomachache.

Mom told me as much as she knew about it before we went. And she cooked stuff like Jell-O and ham salad because she said I wouldn't be able to chew. Also she asked Aunt Mary to ride along in case I needed help while we were driving home. Aunt Mary helps with Uncle Dick's business, so she can take time off pretty much when she wants to.

I was so scared in the waiting room I couldn't do anything except wait. Did You get my message? You must have, because my knees held me up when the nurse called my name.

Was I ever surprised to see Dr. Riggs in that messy green top and pants. I thought dentists always wore smooth white smocks—like a uniform or something. He looked at the papers from my orthodontist and said, "Wow, we'd better get started." I think he was trying to be funny, but I wasn't laughing. In fact, it was all I could do to keep from crying.

The nurses were nice, but nice doesn't help too much in a case like that. One gave me a shot to make me go to sleep, and I felt like the room was going in circles.

"Wake up! Are you awake? Squeeze my fingers. You did just great!"

Who cares? Sorry, I guess You did. But all I could think

of was how much I hurt—my mouth, my nose, my cheeks, my head, even my ears. Somehow Mom and the nurse got a sweater on me, and the next thing I knew I was sitting in the backseat of the car with Aunt Mary.

"I feel like crying," I said.

"Go ahead," my aunt said. "It's OK to cry."

I'm glad it's OK to cry, Lord.

Well, I spent the afternoon curled up on the couch covered with the red afghan. I had pills for the pain and pills to keep away infection. But the best thing was getting to drink milk shakes.

Today I was still on the couch looking just like a chipmunk. Everyone has been treating me so nice. I really feel special and loved. Even by my brothers. Maybe that's one reason we have to go through some of these hard experiences—to feel special and loved, I mean.

However, tonight I felt a different kind of pain. Dad said a ride in the car would do me good. (He just got a new car, and he's like us kids with a new bike!)

Well, he turned the corner, singing at the top of his voice to make me feel good. And then I saw it. A yellow and black For Sale sign in front of Eric Swenson's house!

Dad stopped singing. "I didn't know the Swensons were moving. I wonder where they're going?" He glanced at me.

I didn't know either. I felt as if my life were over before it even began. Would any other boy ever think I'm beautiful?

I had no pill for this newest pain.

8

Panty Hose

Lord, it's me, Jennifer.

Actually, Julie started it. We were all going along the way we always had until the Sunday she showed up in panty hose! I guess we should have expected something like that, since she has a big sister in high school.

But all of a sudden the rest of us felt like babies in our socks. Not that Julie really looked that different. After all, when you have toothpick legs, even nylons don't change them that much. But it *was* hard to concentrate on feeding the five thousand.

It didn't take much to figure out what would happen the next Sunday. Right! Laurie and Lisa showed up in

Sunday school with panty hose on, too. They came in together and smiled at everybody. Julie told them how nice they looked. I didn't say anything. I was trying to keep my mind on what Miss Gregg was saying. She told us that You are just like Jesus. It is easier than ever to talk to You now that I know that.

But still, that just left Kathy and me with our bare knees hanging out. And you know my mother! That's why I casually mentioned to Dad that I was the *only* one in Sunday school without panty hose. It was a good try, and I'm sorry it wasn't really true. But anyhow he wasn't impressed and said what I hoped he wouldn't say, "Ask your mother." As if I haven't been asking for years!

I needed to find the right time to ask her. I knew immediately that dinner wasn't it. Pete and Justin were fighting, and Mom was so upset that she didn't even realize I offered to help set the table without being told. "Is that what you learned in Sunday school?" she asked them.

Of course, sometimes kids do fight in Sunday school, but that wasn't her point, and everyone, even Pete and Justin, knew it. Anyhow, by the time we all sat down to eat, I had even forgotten about my own problem.

"God is just like Jesus," I announced to everyone at the table. My father kept on carving the meat. Nobody said anything and since I hate silence, I decided I might as well tell them some more. "Jesus was followed by 5,000 hungry people who didn't bring lunches along."

"Why not?" Pete asked.

Since I really didn't know, I ignored him.

"What did they do, starve?" asked Justin.

"One boy had a lunch," I explained. "Jesus passed it around and fed everybody. There were even leftovers!"

"Eat your own dinner before it gets cold," Dad said. As You can see, it wasn't the right time to talk about You either.

That evening I got my courage up and told Mom I wanted to ask her something. Compared to the bathing suit, it didn't seem like much, but it was important to me. "Three of the girls in Sunday school are wearing panty hose. Can I start?" I was ready with four good reasons why I should. (Well, three good ones and an extra, just in case.)

Mom actually smiled. "I was wondering when you'd ask again," she said. "I can take you shopping tomorrow while the boys swim. OK?"

OK? I nearly fainted, I was so happy she understood. I guess it was the right time.

The rest of the week I could hardly wait until Sunday morning. When I walked into class, I felt everyone looking at me. Except for Kathy.

After class I stood next to Kathy and acted like I wanted to be her friend. "Panty hose are really not all that great," I said. "I feel just the same."

Kathy said she couldn't care less.

Lord, when it's the right time for Kathy, please help her mother understand!

9

Win Some, Lose Some

Lord, it's me, Jennifer.

You know, I think this may turn out to be the best year of my life! When school first started, I really didn't expect too much. First off, Eric moved away which was a real blow. He'd been my idol since kindergarten, and just when he'd finally started talking to me, off he moved to Houston. Pow! Just like that.

And then to get Lacy for homeroom. Everybody knows that by this grade language arts is supposed to be a breeze, especially for verbal types like me. What would You think if all along You were looking forward to a cinchy year and then, all of a sudden, they changed the rules?

Go directly to jail. Do not pass Go. Do not collect $200.

Instead of reading contests, and fun things, we're diagraming sentences. And we have to write themes every week. I'm sure it's as bad as college. Never before in my life have I actually had homework in language arts. But, like Grandma Andrews always says, "Some things turn out to be blessings in disguise."

The thing is, I've always been verbal. That's Mom's way of saying I talk too much! Which is why I've always wanted to be either a lawyer or an investigative reporter. Of course, lots of people want to be journalists now. Dad says he thinks it started when some newspaper reporters turned out to be the heroes of Watergate. Pete thinks I'm influenced by TV, which is really a put-down, 'cause he isn't even old enough to stay up and watch!

Well, getting back to Miss Lacy, would you ever in a million years guess that Katherine Lacy—with the tie shoes and shirtwaist dresses—would turn out to be a journalist in disguise? Honestly! She told us today that she graduated from the university's school of journalism. She was even an editor on the school newspaper.

Well, maybe You don't get the point. What I'm trying to say is that here I am with a head start on my career. How many girls do You know who get to learn to diagram sentences from a real live journalist? Even if she does wear tie shoes! Now if I can just find a lawyer who teaches social studies.

I was feeling great until I had a hassle with Mom. Just

when I was beginning to think our relationship was going great, I'm very close to hating her! Sometimes I feel as if she never was a girl at all. I can't even imagine what she was like at my age. Probably a lot like Harriet Peats!

My point is, wouldn't a mother who loved her daughter let her get her ears pierced? I wonder if Dad would let me? At the rate I'm going, I'll probably be the only girl in high school without pierced ears. Me and Harriet Peats.

Lord, do You have much influence over mothers?

Also, if I am supposed to be a lawyer, how will I know?

10

Story Problems

Lord, it's me, Jennifer.

It's not that I'm bad at math. Give me a page of regular problems and I hardly ever make a mistake. Math is, after all, just memorizing facts and using common sense. That's why I always find story problems more of a challenge. They have plots that get me sidetracked. I can get really involved in them.

My father, the accounting major, simply doesn't understand why I find it so hard to make what he calls "practical applications." But that's just the point. The stories aren't practical at all!

For instance, would You be interested in some examples from my math review homework?

Problem 1. "Of the 31 students in one classroom, 17 have brown hair. What percent of the students have brown hair?"

Well, if 17 have brown hair, that means that 14 have hair of other colors. And, anyway, how many other colors are there? There's only one real blond in our whole school since Eric moved, unless you count those whose mothers let them use color. So let's say there are four blonds. Black is almost as rare as blond, but let's give them three. That still leaves seven kids whose hair isn't brown, blond, or black. So what color is it?

Problem 2. "Terry, Dave, and George shared a large pizza. Terry ate $\frac{1}{3}$ of it. Dave ate $\frac{1}{4}$ of it, and George ate $\frac{1}{3}$ of it. What part of the pizza was left?"

Being good at fractions, I discover that 1/12 of the pizza was left. But why wasn't Dave hungry enough to eat as much as his friends? OK, so he had a bigger dinner. But wouldn't you think Terry or George could have finished it? After all, 1/12 of even a large pizza couldn't have been more than a few bites. Have You ever seen three guys who couldn't finish a pizza? I haven't.

Problem 3. "There are 198 girls and 270 boys at Johnsonburg Junior High. There are 260 girls and 325 boys at Ames Junior

High. Is the ratio of girls to boys at Johnsonburg equal to the ratio of girls to boys
at Ames?"

Who cares! Just where are those schools anyhow? I'd
like to transfer to either one!

Problem 4. "Jake bought 12 greeting
cards at 35¢ each. How much did they
cost in all?"

Well, let's assume that Jake could still find greeting
cards for 35¢, which I seriously doubt. The last decent
birthday card I bought was twice that, and I'm not talking about the fabulous cards you'd send to somebody
you really liked a lot. So the book hasn't kept up with
inflation! What has! Still, why would one boy, even one
named Jake, buy 12 greeting cards all at one time? Does
he have 12 friends with birthdays in the same month?
Does he plan ahead? Even allowing for grandmothers
and favorite aunts, he'd hardly need that many. Or is
Jake shy? Does he send greeting cards instead of talking
to people—to tell them he likes them, that he's sorry, that
he misses them, etc.? It sure beats me!

Problem 5. "Janice takes dancing lessons.
Thursday she practiced 2 $7/12$ hours. Friday she practiced 1 $9/12$ hours. How long
did she practice in all?"

What I want to know is how she figured out that she practiced 2 $7/12$ hours the first day? And, good grief, with all that practicing, how does she have time to do anything else? Is she a social dropout? Has she turned pro already? Does she have a mean mother who makes her do it? What kind of dancing does she do? Well, here again we have more problems than we started with!

> **Problem 6.** "Paula rode her bicycle to her friend's house in 30 minutes. She walked back home. She rode twice as fast as she walked. How long did it take her to make the round trip?"

I know the answer is an hour and a half. But why did Paula leave her bike at her friend's house? Did it break down? Was she giving it to her friend (unlikely), or lending it to her? Was her friend even a girl? And then there's that long walk home! It took her an hour! Wouldn't her mom come for her? Is she going to be late for supper? If the friend is a boy, do they stroll hand in hand in spring-time beauty, gradually falling in love? *("To think, my darling, we owe this lifetime of bliss to that 10-speed bike!")* Or did Paula's mother meet her at the door with the words, "Where is your bike? Forgot it again, did you? You're grounded for two weeks!"

You probably think I'm making these story problems up, but honestly I'm not. They're all in my math book. And at the rate I'm going, before I'm finished I'll have spent 4 $73/90$ hours at this. I'll have gray hair. Without a bite of pizza in the house, I'll no doubt starve. So if someone can spare 35¢ for a get-well card, please have him ride over with it tomorrow!

11

So Many Points for a Bible

Lord, it's Jennifer again.

As You've probably noticed, Sunday school has become a part of our family's schedule. The Green family as a whole is big on schedules, especially Mom. So Pete has stopped complaining.

I really enjoy my class, and I can't believe how much I'm learning. At first the other girls couldn't believe that I had never even heard of Your prayer or things in the Bible they've been taught all their lives. They thought I was putting them on when I didn't understand their special Sunday vocabulary.

For example, I always thought a "witness" was someone who saw a criminal rob a bank or happened to be on the corner when two cars smashed together. I thought "testimony" was the witness' story at the trial, like on TV. And "rapture" was what you felt when a boy kissed you. And sin—wow—that was murder or robbing or pushing dope. "Grace" was somebody's aunt's name—popular in the olden days before everybody was called Laura or Amy or Jennifer.

Naturally, I don't like to seem stupid, especially in a place like Sunday school! So instead of talking all the time, I have tried to listen a lot more and keep my mouth shut.

I really think the miracles are my favorite things. When we had the story about Jesus walking on the water, I nearly flipped out. Everybody else seemed kinda bored. I mean, like it was everyday stuff! The point of the story was to keep watching Jesus and not look around at what is happening to you. Well, I want to tell You, if I ever see You walking on a lake, You sure aren't going to find *me* looking at anything else!

I think Pete and Justin have adjusted pretty well. Luckily they're in different classes, because they're easier to handle separately. Pete's teacher got his attention right off the bat by telling him that when You want to create something, all You have to do is say the word. No hammers or nails or anything. He was impressed, as You probably realized.

The newest thing at church is "club night" on Tuesdays. I never realized people went to church then, but it's probably even busier than Sunday mornings with more kids there. My brothers like it because they don't have to dress up and especially because there's food.

At first nobody invited me. I had to watch TV or read or something while my brothers got to go. But last week Laurie seemed surprised that I didn't know about club and said I didn't need an invitation. In fact, a number of kids from school go, and they don't even come to Sunday school! Is that OK with You?

Laurie said I could be in her column, whatever that is. At least I'll have a place. Also, she told me we'd get points for bringing shares and a Bible.

"What are shares?" I asked.

"You know, money. Like the collection in Sunday school," she said. I guess it's like dues.

"How much?" I wanted to know.

"Whatever," she said.

Lord, is a dime OK? I'll try to watch to find out how much the others are bringing.

But when it comes to bringing a Bible for points, I wasn't so sure. You know our Bible, Lord. It's the huge book on the coffee table in the living room. I've always thought it was sort of a family heirloom. I decided I'd better ask Mom, points or not.

"Can I take our Bible to the club meeting at church Tuesday night?"

Mom seemed surprised at the idea. "Well, I'll think about it," she said. Then she stopped her needlepoint and gave me her full attention. "Do the other girls take Bibles?"

"Laurie said they do. It sounds like a contest to see which group brings the most." Naturally Mom realizes I'm competitive since she's known me all my life.

"Well, it does seem odd. But I guess it's OK if you think you can carry it without dropping it. I'd hate to have it ruined."

"I'll be careful," I promised.

A lot of the other kids bring small Bibles to Sunday school, and Laurie always shares hers with me when we read something. Well, maybe we'd get extra points for a big Bible like ours!

When Tuesday night came, Laurie's parents picked me up. When they honked, I went for the Bible. It was even heavier than I thought! Laurie's dad had to help me when I got to the door.

"What have we here?" he asked.

I showed him our Bible. It really is beautiful, Lord.

"That's quite a Bible, Jennifer," he said. "Let me help you carry it."

"I think I can manage," I told him, but he did hold it while I got into the car.

"Hi, Jennifer," Laurie said. "You know my parents. They're both club leaders."

Luckily no one else was riding with us—just Laurie, her parents, me, some cupcakes, and my family's Bible. We took up the whole car.

"You take the cupcakes, Janet, and I'll help Jennifer," Laurie's father said. He had the biggest smile I had ever seen.

Well, the Bible was a sensation, to put it mildly. We put it on a table near our group, but we only got one point for it.

As it turned out, at the end of the meeting we had something called Bible X. Our leader, whose name is Mrs. Fuller, told us that the X is just short for "exploration." We each had a verse to look up in our Bibles. The codes were marked on little pieces of paper and handed out to each girl. Mine said, "John 3:16."

I tried to look confident as I walked over to the table to get my Bible. But, to be honest, I didn't have even the slightest idea how to find anything in that big book!

I ran my finger along the beautiful gold edges of the pages. I could hear the other girls flipping the pages in their small Bibles. I decided to say I had to go to the bathroom. But just then Mrs. Fuller appeared by my side.

"May I help you, Jennifer?" she asked as she smiled a loving kind of smile. "This is the most beautiful Bible I have ever seen!" She opened it. "Here we are," she said, pointing to some words written in red letters. "I'll tell you when it's your turn to read."

I stood there looking at the page. *It is The Holy Bible,* I thought. *God's very own book. And I could understand most of the words!*

When Mrs. Fuller signaled to me, I read in a soft voice, "For God so loved the world, that he gave his only begotten Son, that whosoever believeth in him should not perish, but have everlasting life." I thought it was the most wonderful thing I had ever read. Even if I didn't under-stand "begotten." I knew I was included in the "whoso-ever."

As I looked up, some of the girls seemed bored, but I didn't care. I put my slip of paper inside the Bible so I could find the verse again. As the other girls read, I hardly knew what they were saying.

Thinking ahead, I decided to find out what a smaller Bible would cost. After all, there was no use taking chances with our beautiful one (and my back!) every Tuesday night.

But Lord, I'm really glad we have such a beautiful copy of Your words in our home. Just between You and me, I think this is the very first time it was ever opened. What an honor for me to be the first one to read what You said!

12

Confession of a Room Mother

Lord, it's me, Jennifer.

Today I made a big discovery. I never realized before that mothers can feel mixed up and confused and frustrated without any help from us. I thought it was always our fault.

Of course, I couldn't help observing mothers over the years. And I've noticed that mothers are not all alike.

Now take Beth's mother. She has always impressed me. She's a sharp dresser and hates clutter. At her house we always take off our shoes inside the kitchen door. Honestly, that house looks like a model home—one with nobody living in it. Also, Beth's mother keeps up on fashions. She wore designer jeans before Beth had any.

Then there's Susan's mom, who's going to college. She gets involved in her homework and things get so messy, it's hard to find a place to sit down in that house. I don't mean to criticize, but we have to step over the laundry and library books and newspapers and—well, You've probably noticed it Yourself. I don't think the kids help much, but nobody seems to care. I'm the only friend Susan will let come in, which is kind of sad.

Lots of the mothers have careers. That means they go somewhere to work and get paid for it. Lord, what is the difference between a job and a career?

Which brings me to my own mother, the one I've observed the most, since I've known her all my life. That's why it was such a surprise to discover that she has lots of feelings inside.

Probably I should have guessed all this, but I tend to miss clues when it comes to people I more or less take for granted. Naturally I can't help noticing when Mom is crabby, or when she gives us disapproving looks. But mostly she seems pretty normal. Strict, but normal.

Our house operates with lots of *rules*. One *rule* is that the living room is never supposed to be messy. The big advantage of that is I can always bring a friend home and count on at least that room to look "presentable," as Mom says. Personally, my own room is a disaster, but Mom doesn't get on my case about it. She just shuts the door.

Well, I'm still trying to decide whether to become a lawyer or a journalist. And when I got home from volleyball, I made my usual stop in the kitchen. Mom was making peanut-butter cookies. Because I have so much language arts homework, I announced that I had finally decided to be a lawyer.

Justin walked in just then. "What do you want to be when you grow up, Mom?" he asked.

"I *am* grown up," Mom said softly. In fact, the very softness of her voice was what made me feel that this was something big.

"That was stupid," I said, as Justin ran outside. "He didn't mean to hurt your feelings or anything. He just wasn't thinking."

"Right," Mom said, not quite as softly. "No one seems to think about me as a person at all. I'm just a cook and a laundry sorter and a body behind the wheel of the car."

I had to admit she had a point. "But you do lots of other things," I said. "And we've always appreciated having you for a room mother at school."

"Right," said Mom again. "There aren't very many mothers at home any more. So who gets to head up the cookie drive? Who gets to drive in the car pool? Who gets everybody else's kids after school?"

"Well," I said, "don't you like to do all that stuff?"

"Usually," she said.

"But not today?" I asked.

"Sometimes," Mom said, looking straight at me, "I get tired of being taken for granted. I feel like nobody appreciates me. And I feel fat and tired and dumb."

I couldn't believe my ears. You know how pretty Mom

is. But I guess it is a long time from one Mothers' Day until the next.

"What would you like to do if you weren't a mother?" I asked.

"That's just the trouble," she replied. "I don't even know. The courses I took in college didn't prepare me to do anything special. And I've always wanted to be a mother."

Well, she does have a problem. I'm glad I'm learning to hug, 'cause it was the only solution I could think of at the moment. It did seem to help. At least Mom began to smile. "I'm sorry I complained," she said, as she went back to pressing fork marks on top of the cookies.

"Mom," I said, "I really do appreciate you. And I know the rest of the family does, too."

"I know that, Jennifer. I'm just feeling mixed up and confused and frustrated today. As Grandma Andrews always says, 'Tomorrow will be better.'"

Well, Lord, to see my mother this way was quite an experience. Can You help her with her problems? As You know, I'm having a hard enough time getting my own act together.

13

My Locker Sticks

Lord, it's me, Jennifer.

Today I was late for social studies class because my locker stuck. I couldn't understand why, because it seemed perfectly OK when I hung my coat up this morning. (Sometimes lockers stick when you have a mess on the floor, but I wasn't guilty.) Finally, I was so desperate I just kicked it, and it popped right open.

I learned about kicking stuff from my father, the handyman. He's very good at building things like bookcases or chair rails. (Chair rails are boards that get nailed up around dining rooms so you don't have to buy as much wallpaper, since they keep the paper from going all the way down to the floor). Well, hammer-and-nail projects are Dad's favorite. He even put up the paneling in our basement.

What Dad isn't good at is repairing. Not that he doesn't try. Sometimes he spends all Saturday driving back and forth to Sears. He claims it's bad luck. If there's ever a screw missing from a package, that's the one he gets. His plumbing, I don't think You want to hear about.

Well, Dad didn't actually kick the humidifier, 'cause it's too high up and he isn't that athletic. But I'm getting ahead of myself. Last Thursday, in the middle of the night, we heard this loud, steady shriek all through the house. I grabbed my pink sweater 'cause I thought it was the fire alarm. (The sweater isn't warm, as You know, but it is my newest one.)

In the hall, I nearly ran into Dad, who was racing for the stairs in his bathrobe. He thought the car horn was stuck. The boys caught up with me in the front hall.

Mom passed us on her way to the basement. She knew the noise was the humidifier. The same thing had happened last week when we were all in school and Dad was in Peapack, New Jersey.

Finally Dad came inside and found the whole family in the basement.

"It's the humidifier," Mom told him. "Just pound on it and it will stop."

"That's no way to fix things," my father said. He went for his screwdriver.

"Anybody seen my screwdriver?" he yelled.

Well, it turned out that Pete was using it for a science

project. And it took him a little while to go and get it. There we all stood at 3:20 A.M. in our pajamas with this piercing sound blasting off! I started to giggle.

"Not funny," said Dad. Finally he got the front off the green box and looked inside. I thought he acted like he had never seen the inside before. (It turned out I was right, only he didn't let on at all. After all, we were there watching.) He poked a few things, unscrewed a few more, but the noise continued. "Maybe I should shut off the water first," he shouted.

"No," Mom shouted back. "Remember the last time you did that?"

Dad remembered.

"I'm going back to bed," Justin said. He's a kid who can sleep through anything. And often does.

When Dad's face started getting red, Mom pulled over a stool from the corner, stood on it, and pounded on the side of the humidifier with her fist. The noise stopped.

"How did you do that?" my dad shouted. He didn't seem to notice that the noise had stopped.

"That's how I fixed it last week," said Mom.

Well, on Saturday Dad spent all day going back and forth to Sears. He bought $16.13 worth of parts, had the water turned off four times, and at 5:30 pronounced the humidifier "fixed."

We were eating supper last night when the noise started blasting off again. Dad calmly excused himself, went downstairs, and we heard this loud pounding. The noise stopped.

"Very unprofessional," he said, when he returned to the table. "Call a repairman tomorrow."

We all started to laugh, and Dad joined in.

Well, back to social studies. I really couldn't concentrate on Swiss exports today, even though Switzerland is my favorite country. I kept wondering if I'd be able to get my coat out of my locker.

After class I bravely walked up to it, lifted the handle, and the locker opened.

At least lockers don't cause trouble in the middle of the night. But I do sort of hate having this thing hanging over my head all the time. So I guess I'll report my problem to Mr. Walker. After all, as my dad says, kicking things isn't very professional.

14

Arnold's Note

Lord, it's me, Jennifer.

I've never been able to make up my mind about Arnold Pelikan. He has always been a puzzle to me. In first grade I thought he was the worst kid in the room. I'm sure he was the one who started the boys trying to pull up our skirts. Was he? Also, Eric was really my idol. But You know how idols are. They never say anything at all to anybody!

Well, I guess I've always admired girls who could treat boys like "real persons." I think some of them have older brothers and are used to boys more than I am. In my case, as You know, Pete and Jus are younger. They've never really been persons. At least not to me. My Andrews cousins are wonderful. They're persons! The only trouble is that they don't seem to think of me as a person!

Back to Arnold Pelikan. By fifth grade I realized that he was really smart. And I've always been attracted to smart people, even boys. That's probably when I started liking him. Sure, Eric was handsome, but it was getting harder to keep caring about him when he never talked to me. And sometimes he got low grades besides! Straight-A Arnold was such a big secret that I never even told Beth. And, as You may know, there wasn't much I didn't tell Beth in fifth grade. I guess there were two good reasons I had trouble admitting I liked Arnold. The first was that nobody (well, almost nobody) admitted they liked a boy, even secretly. The second reason was his name.

I know it isn't fair not to like somebody because of his name. But Arnold Pelikan is an exception. In my mind, at least. I could hardly admit, even to myself, that I liked somebody named Pelikan, smart or not. If it struck me funny while I secretly liked him, what about the girls who didn't? They'd have laughed me right out of the sixth grade!

Well, this year it's becoming clear that girls and boys are really noticing each other as persons. In fact, Lord, that's all Beth and I secretly talk about. (Brad even stood by Lynn's locker the other day!)

Probably You can imagine my surprise when I found this note stuck right in my social studies workbook. I've memorized it. "I like you very much. Signed, Arnold Pelikan."

I was too embarrassed to glance over at him. And anyhow when I did, he was looking the other way. So I stared at the pictures of mountains in my book and concentrated hard on the list of natural resources, but at the end of class I couldn't remember a single one. And I'm pretty smart, too! If that's bragging, no offense!

What if Arnold wanted to walk me home? What if he came and stood by my locker and I had to kick it? Would Arnold offer to kick it for me? And worst of all, if I married him, I'd forever be named Jennifer Pelikan!

Well, Lord, after all that, Arnold walked out of social studies with Tom and Matthew and pretended he didn't even see me.

I've decided not to tell Beth or Laurie or Sarah. And I sure hope You can keep a secret!

15

Christmas Present

Lord, it's Jennifer again.

For at least two years I've wanted a horse. Which is kind of funny when you think about it, 'cause we don't even have a dog!

Mom just isn't big on pets. She says we don't have room for a dog to run. And, regardless of what the boys say, she insists that she'd be the one stuck with taking care of it, which is probably true.

Of course, with a horse it's different. Horses don't wet on the floor or chew up furniture or need walking at 10 P.M. And they are so beautiful and romantic.

Well, for two years Dad and Mom have pointed out that the nearest stable is miles away. I wish they weren't so right! It makes it hard to answer their arguments. But I just know that if you want something so much, there has to be a way. Doesn't there?

This year we turned in our Christmas lists the day after Thanksgiving, like we always do. The only thing I asked for was a horse. And nobody has said a word about it. That could mean only one thing!

We open our family presents on Christmas morning. But for years Pete and Jus and I have had a secret pact. Whoever wakes up first wakes the other kids. Then we sneak down and look under the tree. Of course, we don't open anything. We just shake and feel and guess. Then we go back to bed.

Dad always brags to everybody that we are such thoughtful kids on Christmas morning. While other parents are awakened at the crack of dawn, the Green kids stay quietly in their beds until 7:30 when Dad puts on his bathrobe and starts singing, "Joy to the World."

That's the signal, and we all get together in our robes to open the presents. This year I was so excited I couldn't get back to sleep after our early scouting expedition. There were almost no presents under the tree for me, except the ones from my brothers. You can always tell theirs because they do their own wrapping!

First, *traditionally,* we check out our stockings. We always get the same things: a whole package of chocolate chips, new toothbrushes and toothpaste, pecans in their shells, an orange, and a small surprise box. Mine contained a gold chain with a single pearl on it.

Well, then everybody started opening gifts. Everybody, that is, except me. I was getting more and more excited. So far all I had gotten was new stretch jeans. Finally Dad announced, with his big grin, that Santa had brought some special treats this year. Oh, wow!

Dad left the room and came back with a thin package for Mom. She opened it and found a watch with diamonds all around it. "Peter, it's too much!" she gasped.

"Not for my special girl," he said. "You deserve even better!"

"Rob a bank?" asked Justin.

"Nope," said Dad. "Big bonus!"

"Now, it's Justin's turn," announced Dad, leaving the room again. He wheeled in a bike. "No more waiting to fit Pete's old one," he said.

"Cosmic!" yelled Jus. Nobody in the family mentions that he is much smaller than Pete was at his age. You've probably noticed, Lord.

"And for Pete, ta daaaa." Dad returned this time with a Schwinn 10-Speed.

"All right!" Pete rushed up to claim his prize. I couldn't help remembering that I didn't get my 10-speed until I was eleven.

"And for the head of the house, my own little toy." It was a home computer.

All this time I was waiting. Finally, Dad looked at me and winked. "Some gifts can't fit under the tree," he said. I could hardly stand it. I decided to name the horse Snap.

"Jennifer," Mom said, "we're getting you a new bedroom set! You can pick it out at the store. And you can decorate with wallpaper, curtains, and a bedspread. A whole new bedroom!"

"A whole new pad," Pete corrected.

"Well," said Dad, still grinning, "how about that, Jennifer? A whole new pad!"

To tell the truth, I hardly heard most of what Mom said. Have you ever cried and laughed at the same time? The tears were rolling down my cheeks. No horse. No Snap. I ran over to hug Mom and Dad. I didn't want them to know how disappointed I was.

Well, we had our *traditional* coffee-cake breakfast and got dressed for church. As You've probably noticed, it is just about the only time Dad and Mom go. It did feel nice to sit together and sing the carols. This year I listened to the preacher. He said You came to earth as the baby Jesus. No wonder You're alike!

In the afternoon we went to our *traditional* Christmas dinner at Aunt Mary's and Uncle Dick's. They think Grandma Andrews has fixed enough turkeys in her lifetime. Sarah's family comes too, but the other Green families live too far away. Sarah gave me what I thought was a regular book, but she said it's a special Bible that's easy to understand. I gave her a blue sweater that my parents paid for.

By late afternoon when Matthew and Joshua asked Sarah and me to play Clue with them, I'd almost forgotten about the horse. I can't even ride a horse. That's how stupid I am.

16

First Snowfall

Lord, it's me, Jennifer.

I am trying hard not to be such a weather person. A weather person is someone who's up or down depending on whether there's sunshine, rain, gloomy days, etc. I've noticed that many weather people are adults, so maybe it's catching!

Well, as You know, this isn't really our first snow. But I don't count it when you hardly have to wear boots. Do You?

What I mean is, this is the first deep snow, the kind that makes me feel excited. Like a birthday or Christmas or a package from Aunt Mary when it isn't even my birthday.

I will admit that boots are a pain. However, they're honestly worth it when the snow comes nearly up to their tops. This time the drifts are so high they would come *over* their tops! Just between You and me, I really do hate getting my feet wet, even though that's something mothers are supposed to worry about.

Anyhow, this snow today is the kind that sometimes means school will be closed early! And You'll have to admit that that's a great unexpected gift. Everyone knows we'll have certain holidays off. But snow days are always a surprise. Are You surprised? Or do You send them just when things are getting boring?

Anyway, I think snow is one of the most beautiful things in the world! Which is kind of amazing, because sometimes I get tired of white paper, or white underwear, or white blouses, or white sheets. But I never get tired of white snow! In fact, when it comes down in big flakes, like today, it colors absolutely everything else white, too—red hats, and dirty streets, and bare branches.

Well, thanks for the beautiful snow today, Lord. I suppose some people will have a hard time because of it—shoveling, getting stuck, missing appointments, even having accidents. Please take care of them. But, personally, I think this is the most wonderful thing You've done all week!

17

New Girl

Lord, it's me, Jennifer.

Today we got a new girl in our Sunday-school class. At least I think she's going to be in the class. Her name is Michelle, and she told us she was "just visiting."

"Where do you live?" Lisa asked her.

"We live here," said Michelle. "We moved here from California. Our furniture hasn't arrived yet so we're staying in a motel."

"Then how come you're a visitor?" I asked.

"Oh," said Michelle smiling, "we always have to check out the churches to find the one Dad likes best."

Just then our teacher came back in.

"Welcome," said Miss Gregg, smiling.

"Hi! I'm Michelle Stacy. We're moving here from California."

"You wouldn't happen to be William Stacy's daughter?" Miss Gregg wondered.

"You've got it!" Michelle smiled all the time.

"I went to college with your brother, Jim. Is he still at home?"

"Nope. Married Ginny Carlson last year. They live in Boston."

"Ginny Carlson!" Miss Gregg was excited. "We were roommates our sophomore year."

Well, all this talk was getting boring to the rest of us. "Big deal," I whispered to Lisa.

"I'm sorry, Class," said Miss Gregg, suddenly realizing the rest of us were there. "Michelle, this is Jennifer, Lisa, Kathy, Susan, and Laurie." As she said our names we each nodded or smiled. "We can talk more later, Michelle."

Then Miss Gregg stopped acting like a girl and started acting like a teacher. "Today's lesson is found in Luke 15. I'm sure you've heard of the prodigal son."

Everyone nodded except me.

"Now what does *prodigal* mean?" Miss Gregg asked.

"Somebody who gets tired of life at home and splits?" Laurie sounded like she was guessing. Could You tell, too?

Miss Gregg looked around the circle.

"A big spender," Michelle smiled. She didn't even have a book!

"Correct," Miss Gregg smiled back. "The younger son in the story took his share of his father's money and wasted it in another country. How many have read the lesson?"

Everybody except Julie and Michelle raised their hands. "But I know the story," said Julie. And Michelle obviously did, too. So how come I was the only one who hadn't heard of the prodigal son? I peeked in my book, but couldn't find *prodigal* mentioned anywhere. *Ran away...hungry...sorry...came home...not prodigal.* It was discouraging. I was trying so hard.

"Well," continued Miss Gregg after we reviewed the story, "I want you to think about the two sons. Are you like either of them?"

I thought. *The younger one? I've never even thought of running away, much less spending my father's money like he did! And I've never been really hungry.*

And how would my father react? Throw a party? No way! He'd probably ground me for the rest of the year! Nope, I'm certainly not like the younger son.

I guess then I must be like the older son who stuck around, didn't make waves, followed the rules. That's me. To tell the truth, I don't think the father in the story was fair!

I realized I was the only one still thinking. Everyone else looked sort of bored, except Michelle. I guess You noticed. "OK, Class," said Miss Gregg. "How many are like the younger son?"

Everybody except me raised their hands. I could hardly

believe it! I've known Laurie all her life almost, and she's never run away or wasted money either. Michelle I'm not sure about.

Miss Gregg didn't ask me why I didn't raise my hand. She just continued the lesson. "Jesus told us this story to show that God is forgiving and loving. No matter what we do, He will welcome us back."

It was time for Sunday school to be over.

"Hope to see you next week, Michelle," said Miss Gregg.

"Thanks," Michelle answered. "I've enjoyed being here." Then she stood up. "I have to meet my family," she said and left alone.

"Her father is William Stacy," Laurie whispered.

"Who's that?" I asked.

"He's famous."

"What for?" I needed to get my brothers.

"I'm not sure," Laurie said. "But he's a Christian leader."

"Like Moses?"

"Don't be silly," Laurie answered. She looked a little angry.

"I thought maybe he was running for God." I mean really!

"Jennifer, that's gross." Laurie was shocked all right.

"Sorry," I muttered. "I have to get going."

"See you tomorrow," she called after me.

"I guess so," I mumbled. It was the first time I didn't like Sunday school very much.

18

Michelle's First Day in School

Lord, it's me, Jennifer.

First thing on Monday, we have homeroom. We've been trying to decide where to go on our spring field trip. The boys want Hawaii, probably because of the grass skirts and hula dances. I'll have to admit the other ideas sound dull in comparison.

Well, right in the middle of everything, the door opened and in walked Michelle Stacy—suntan, short blond hair, warm smile.

The room went up for grabs! The boys whistled and cheered, and the girls just sat there. Of course, Laurie and I were the only ones who knew who she was. I managed to wave when she glanced my way, but she wasn't really looking at anyone special. Like me on the Betsy Ross float.

Miss Lacy isn't one for letting things get out of hand. And the boys know it. So, when she narrowed her eyes and looked around the room, everything got still. Deathly still.

Michelle handed Miss Lacy some papers and waited while she looked at them.

"Class, I'd like you to meet Michelle Stacy, who has just moved here from Santa Barbara, California. You've already welcomed her adequately. Michelle, you may sit in the second row."

"Yes, ma'am." Every eye followed her to the second row. I suppose You noticed. Or do You stick to Sunday school?

"Now, where were we?"

"Hawaii," said Arnold Pelikan, "but *now* who needs it?" Everyone laughed except the girls.

I started feeling kinda sorry for her. The boys act brave as a group, but most of them are too chicken to even talk to a girl. As for the girls, Michelle would be competition.

After homeroom we went right into language arts, which is one of my favorite classes. Miss Lacy may be tough, but she knows how to teach! I've learned more in her class than any I've ever had. I got to read my short story in front of the class—the one about Christmas *traditions* in my family. Everybody laughed at the part about Justin throwing icicles so Mom would scream.

As we headed out for math class, I waited for Michelle.

"Hi," I said, smiling at her.

Michelle smiled back.

"The first day is always the hardest," I told her. Then I wondered if she had someone like Grandma Andrews to teach her that kind of stuff.

"Right," she agreed.

"I'm Jennifer," I reminded her.

"Nice to meet you," she said.

"We met yesterday," I reminded her. "In Sunday school."

"Of course," she smiled. "Sorry. Everything is so confused. I'll be glad when we get settled. Our furniture is coming tomorrow."

"Where's your house?" We walked toward the math room.

"On Oak Street," she said. "I can't remember the number. We move so much it's hard to keep everything straight. It makes you feel stupid when you can't even remember your phone number."

"Gosh," I said. "We've never moved. I can't even imagine what it would be like. Did you happen to buy Eric's house?"

Michelle looked blank.

"Yellow colonial with black shutters?"

"We must have. Who was Eric?"

"Oh," I tried to sound casual, "just a boy I've known all my life. The Swensons moved to Houston a long time ago. You're only a couple of blocks from me."

"That's nice," Michelle said. She stopped smiling.

"Here I go again with my transfer papers." She stood at Miss Adamson's desk, and I took my seat.

Now that it was over, I was glad I'd decided to be friendly. After all, a new person needs at least one friend. Right?

After school Mom picked me up and we went to the furniture store to pick out stuff for my room. Green's Furniture is sort of a family thing. Grandpa Green had it first, and Uncle Bob took over when Grandpa and Grandma retired. Dad wasn't interested since he's a sales engineer. But we get furniture at half price anyway because we're *family*.

"Why don't we just look around and get ideas today," Mom said. "Then you can think about it. It's usually a good idea to take your time on important purchases."

Did Grandma Andrews tell her that? "Sounds good," I agreed.

All the bedroom furniture is in one section. Some of the area is curtained off to look like little bedrooms. Still, it's hard to imagine anything in my own room.

"Do you like this?" Uncle Bob joined us. "It's a new line that's been advertised in lots of magazines."

What I liked was the wallpaper. It was white with little blue designs. I love blue and white! "Mom, can I have that wallpaper?"

"Well, Jennifer, usually it's better to pick out the wallpaper later. "Are there rules for everything in life, Lord?

"Can I get a desk?" I wondered.

"Maybe it would save space to get a desk top with

drawers underneath," Mom said. "This style has a whole set of storage pieces that fit together. Like it?"

I looked at the unit. There were shelves, drawers, desks, cabinets—places for everything. I could imagine myself arranging my books and my collections. Maybe I could even become neat! My own private little apartment. My own pad!

"Canopy bed?" I suggested. (Susan has one that I like a lot.)

"If you're sure that's what you want," Mom said. "It's your room!"

I was beginning to get excited. "Can we buy it today?"

"I still think it would be better to wait a day or two. We can measure all the walls and make sure we get the right sizes. Do you like the white finish or the natural wood?"

"Gosh, I don't know!"

"Well, I'd say you have a great start, Jennifer. Would you like to stop for a coke?"

Well, this was special! I suggested a spot where none of the kids go—just in case.

"Her name is Michelle Stacy," I finished telling Mom. "I kinda feel sorry for her moving so much."

"That's nice of you, Jennifer. If you want to have friends, you have to be friendly."

"I know, Mom. Grandma Andrews! Right?" I finished my drink.

"Mom," I said suddenly, "do you think I'd look pretty with short hair?"

19

Stacys Move In

Lord, it's Jennifer again.

After school today Laurie and I walked home together. We decided to detour a block so we could see Michelle's family moving in. When we were little we used to sit on the grass and watch the moving vans unload. Naturally, we don't do that anymore. Today was too cold anyway. But we thought we might see more of the Stacy family.

"I'm getting the dark wood," I told Laurie. "I think the white looks too babyish." I saw the look on her face and knew I was in trouble. "I mean, when you pick out a bedroom set for yourself . . ." My voice trailed off.

Laurie didn't say anything. I didn't want to hurt her feelings or sound like I was bragging. Oh, crumb! I decided to try again. "What I'm really excited about is choosing wallpaper. Hope I can find one I like as much as yours!" Whew.

"Well," Laurie answered, "I do like mine. Have you decided on a color?"

"Probably blue and white," I said. "Maybe a check or plaid."

"My mom says Laura Ashley prints are 'in.'"

"What's that?" I asked.

"You know, little, kind of old-fashioned patterns. Some have matching material for curtains and bedspreads."

"I'll look them up," I promised.

Just then we saw the van. It was the biggest one I'd ever seen—nearly half a block long. Uniformed men were carrying things covered in blankets down a ramp from an opening in the middle. "Ready for the sofa?" one man called.

Michelle was nowhere in sight. A woman wearing a coat stood inside the open front door. Each moving man would say something to her as he passed, and she would answer. She looked cold.

"Well," said Laurie, "I hope they enjoy living here."

"Why wouldn't they?" I wondered.

"Oh, I don't know. It's just that they've been in some special places."

"What's so special about California? Personally, I'd hate to live in a place that never had snow." I felt very loyal to Illinois.

"It isn't just California. They've lived all over the world!" Laurie was obviously impressed.

"You're putting me on!" I wasn't about to fall for that. "And my mom has never heard of them!" I continued. "Some famous!"

"Well," said Laurie, "I'm not putting you on. My dad and mom said the Stacys moved to California from South America. They were with TSAL."

"What's that?" I asked.

"A literature mission," Laurie explained.

"Sounds like a diet," I laughed.

"No kidding," Laurie continued. "They spent time with KOOM."

"I know," I said, "a rock group!"

"Wrong," she laughed. "But you're close. It's a radio station."

"In South America?"

"No, South Africa. But they had to leave."

"Nobody liked the music?" I guessed.

"No. It wasn't safe there any longer."

"I suppose they've lived in Switzerland," I said, hoping they hadn't. Lord, I consider that my country.

"Well, they didn't live there. But Mr. Stacy did head up CEEME."

"Another missionary group?" I asked.

"Nope," Laurie said slowly, "the Conference on Eastern European Mission Endeavors. Dad says they meet every three years. Last time was in Geneva."

"For all this, the guy's famous?" I wondered.

"Not really," Laurie admitted. "Dad says he's written theology books. And he writes regularly for *CM*. Sometimes they quote him in *Newsweek*."

"Oh," I said. "*Newsweek* I've heard of. What's *CM?*"

"*Christian Monthly,*" said Laurie, "but everybody calls it *CM.*"

"So that's how Michelle's dad got famous!"

"Well, partly," Laurie continued. "In California he was the acting president of a college."

"I'm beginning to realize Mr. Stacy isn't known for his surfing ability," I said.

"Almost correct," said Laurie. "In college he was a star baseball player. He had a chance to play for the Phillies."

"I can't believe it!" I said. "Why didn't he?"

"He wanted to go into FCS." Now even Laurie was starting to laugh.

"I'm not even going to ask!" I teased. "Enough! And what is the famous Mr. Stacy going to do here?"

"My parents don't know," Laurie said. "And it's Dr. Stacy now."

Lord, do You have Your own code book?

20

Second Best

Lord, it's me, Jennifer.

The more I've gotten into fixing up my room, the more I've been able to forget the disappointment in not getting a horse for Christmas. Like every day it hurts less. But I'll never stop wanting a horse.

I guess You've noticed that Dad's been spending more and more time away from home. He used to be gone overnight only a couple of times a month. Lately he's been gone several days a week to the East coast.

It's hard to put into words how different things are when Dad's gone. He is basically a fun person and always joking. Although I'll have to admit that some of his puns are awful.

Why is it that everybody in the family acts different when he's gone? Mom fixes simple meals. That usually means something easy or a casserole nobody likes. She tackles stuff like cleaning the oven or sorting out spring clothes to see what still fits. Also she reads a lot.

I think the boys miss Dad most. Mom yells at them a lot. And they seem to fight more. Although I call them "the boys," they are very different. Pete is a loner; his one and only friend is named Joseph. Their idea of fun is getting archeology books out of the library. Justin is small for his age but makes up for it by being quick and well-coordinated in sports. He has lots of friends.

The things I miss most about Dad are his fairness and his sparkle. In fact, when Dad's gone it's like ginger ale without any fizz.

Today Mom took me to the furniture store for the big order. Uncle Bob said I could have the display pieces if he had what I wanted. Except for the canopy bed, everything was in stock. I picked out a wall unit that includes a desk, bookcases, drawers for my clothes, and a cabinet with doors—all in brown wood. Uncle Bob said it will take at least a month to get the bed. I'm glad I don't have to wait for everything!

Are You familiar with wallpaper books? They're about as heavy as our family Bible! I've seen Mom look through whole stacks. The idea is to put markers in the pages you like most. Otherwise it's impossible to find them again!

Mom and I stopped to pick up three wallpaper books

including a Laura Ashley. I spent almost all evening watching TV and trying to decide. Picturing a whole room of any pattern is very hard for me. I think it's even worse than choosing fabric for a dress or blouse.

I think Mom is trying hard to let me do the choosing instead of telling me what she likes. Now if I just knew what I liked! One paper had horses all over it. Don't think I wasn't tempted!

"He's doing it again!" Pete yelled.

"Stop it!" Mom yelled back. The door slammed and we could hear the boys wrestling.

"I think they need separate rooms," Mom said. She talks to me when Dad's gone.

"Which do you like best?" I asked Mom. "I mean, of these three wallpapers?"

She put down her book kinda grudgingly. I turned to the pages with my markers.

"Ummmm," Mom said, looking at a blue and white plaid.

"Ummmm," she said, looking at a blue and white Laura Ashley print.

"Ummmm," she said, looking at a paper that had big blue stencils.

"Well?" I asked.

"Looks as if you've decided on blue!" I don't really think she was surprised. "Your room isn't very large," she reminded me. "Usually smaller patterns work out better in smaller areas."

"So the stencils are out?" I asked.

"Either of the others would be lovely," Mom said. "Maybe Dad can paint your woodwork Saturday."

"No kidding?"

"He said he'll try if he isn't too tired."

"I think I'll get the Laura Ashley," I decided, "with white curtains and spread and canopy."

"You have expensive taste!" Mom smiled. "But good taste."

"Is it too much?" I backed off. "I don't want to waste Dad's money."

"No, Jennifer. No problem. Let's measure the space and get the paper ordered."

Dad got home Friday night. Instead of looking tired, he looked excited.

"Great to be home!" he announced. "I hear I'm scheduled to do a little painting."

"Oh, rats," Justin said. "I was hoping you'd coach me in soccer."

"Maybe Sunday," Dad said. "Want to join us, Pete?"

"Not really," Pete replied. "I'm never going to be any good at sports."

"You're right, Pete." Dad said. "With an attitude like that, you'll never improve. Couldn't you just try?"

"I have other plans," Pete said. It sounded to me like a lie.

21

Forgotten Book

Lord, it's me, Jennifer.

I really believe You understand, Lord. But for kids who have parents that don't care, what happened to me today would sound like something from outer space. As You know, my parents do care. Which means I'm supposed to do my homework, if I have any, without involving them.

As they have explained to us, we all have our responsibilities. Dad goes to work whether he feels like it or not. Mom cooks, cleans, shops—stuff like that. And we kids do our homework. It is called *responsibility.*

Even Justin has learned this. He's kind of a flake at math— much to Dad's dismay—so he wouldn't dare ask Dad for help. Mom must have been bad at math, too, 'cause she's sympathetic. Not that it helps Justin. She tells him she's "paid her dues." I think that means she suffered through it once, and once was enough!

Well, to get to my point, yesterday I forgot to bring home my social studies book.

"Are you coming to basketball practice?" Lisa wanted to know.

"Coming," I answered.

Well, basketball was exhausting. Lisa's sister says you get used to it, but so far I haven't. And to make things even worse, I didn't play well. Plus I skinned my knee when I tried for a ball going out of bounds.

I was nearly all the way home when I remembered I was supposed to read the next chapter in social studies for class discussion. Mom wasn't home because she was picking up Justin at a friend's, and I knew the school would be locked by the time I got back. Plus then I'd be late for dinner.

In short, I knew I was in trouble.

Usually I talk a lot at dinner, but last night I just listened. (Justin is going out for Little League, which obviously pleased Dad. No, Pete isn't going out for Little League, which obviously did not please Dad.) Nobody praised Mom's new recipe. (Justin's "Yuck" nearly got him sent to his room!) And Dad said he'd be on the East coast for three days. I was so quiet Mom asked if I felt OK. I said I did, but it wasn't true.

After supper I called Lisa. She wasn't even home. Linda was home, but she was using her social studies book. She has parents who check up: "Do you have homework? How much? What are you supposed to do?" Finally Dad said I couldn't use the phone any longer. He was expecting a call.

Well, I tried to watch TV, but I felt so guilty. I read a library book, filed my nails, took a warm bath, and went to bed early. Then Mom was so sure I was sick she took my temperature. Of course, it was normal!

As You know, I considered faking illness. It did cross my mind briefly, but I'd miss out on too much, including club.

On the way to school Beth noticed how quiet I was. "What's wrong?" she asked.

See, when I'm quiet, everybody thinks something's wrong!

"I forgot to take my social studies home."

"That's it?" Beth asked. She couldn't believe it.

"She'll call on me and I won't know the answer."

"So?"

"So she'll know I didn't read it."

"Good grief, Jennifer!"

Well, that's all right for her to say. She isn't *responsible*.

Sometimes there's time to study during other classes, but not today. It was time for lunch before I knew it, and social studies comes right after lunch. I could hardly eat.

I took a deep breath before I entered the room. I couldn't decide whether to look at Mrs. Plemmons or not. I decided I wouldn't.

90

I slipped into my seat and opened my book. As I flipped through Switzerland I noticed the mountains didn't look as pretty as they had before. By the time I found the place, there was no time to read. The bell rang.

"Well, Class," a strange voice began. "Mrs. Plemmons is ill today."

I looked up at the substitute.

"You can have the class period today to complete your study of France. Be prepared for a test on Wednesday."

As she finished speaking Daniel Casey sounded forth with one of his long, repulsive, thoroughly-disgusting belches. The class dissolved in laughter.

And today I think I laughed louder than anyone in the class.

22

Exit
the Handyman

Lord, it's Jennifer again.

The wallpaper store called to tell us my paper was in. I could hardly wait to see it, so Mom and I drove out to pick it up before supper.

"Dad, want to see my wallpaper?" I hit him with it the minute he walked in the door which was bad timing.

My father's big grin had drooped to a thin-lipped smile. "Hi, Jennifer. Not now, please."

With split-second timing, Justin bounded in all sweaty from soccer practice. "I made the team! Dad, I did it!" he yelled.

"Wonderful," said Dad so slowly that I could hear every syllable. "Tell me about it at supper, OK?"

"Peter, is that you?" Mom stuck her head around the kitchen door. "I think the water softener is going out. The clothes are a mess."

"Sue, can it wait?" Dad finished hanging his coat in the hall closet and dropped into his chair in the living room.

Almost immediately the front door opened again. Pete smiled. "Hi, Dad!"

"Hi! Pete, would you get me a Pepsi?"

"Sure, Dad. Just a minute." He threw his coat over a chair and headed for the kitchen.

"Here you are, Peter William Green. At your service!" Pete said to Dad.

"Thanks, Peter William Green, Jr!" Dad said. Then he sipped on the Pepsi.

"Hard day?" asked Pete.

"Unreal," said Dad. "How 'bout you?"

"Same."

"Join me," Dad invited.

Pete left, returned shortly with a glass. Neither talked. I could hear the ice cubes clink in the glasses. Justin had blown on upstairs. Mom was back in the kitchen. I stood quietly in the hall.

I don't know how to explain it, but suddenly I realized how self-centered we all are. I come home every night to toot my own little horn, and the others do the same. Yet somehow the clinking ice spoke to me of a family togetherness that I hadn't felt before. Father and son were just being together. No words were needed.

Suddenly, I felt like an intruder. I tiptoed upstairs to my room.

With Dad out of town so much, there just wasn't enough of him to go around when he was home. His do-it-yourself projects almost stopped.

"Why don't you get somebody to hang Jennifer's wallpaper?" he suggested to Mom. "I just don't have the time."

The somebody turned out to be two housewives. And they did a nice job, too. Everything matched right (Mom is very particular about matching), and my room looked entirely different.

When the new furniture was delivered, Uncle Bob took my old stuff in his truck to the resale shop. He gave me a frame for the new box springs and mattress so they won't have to sit on the floor until the canopy bed arrives.

It's taking me a long time to get everything in the right drawers and cabinets, but it's kind of fun. I even threw out some stuff I have been saving since about fourth grade. We put my bulletin board on the back of the door, and I'm arranging my souvenirs and birthday cards and pictures of horses. My record player fits into one cabinet. And even without the new curtains and what Mom calls finishing touches, it is one of the prettiest rooms I've ever seen.

I decided two things: I will always keep it looking nice, and I will always keep wanting a horse anyhow!

23

Michelle Settles In

Lord, it's Jennifer again.

Michelle Stacy was back in our Sunday-school class the third week. "This is where God wants us," she announced.

I wanted to ask her how she knew. But there was no use taking a chance on looking stupid. Lord, do Christian leaders have special ways of finding out stuff like that?

"We're glad to have you join us," Miss Gregg said. She gave her a lesson book and wrote Michelle's name in the attendance book. "Can I have your address and phone number?"

"It's 1730 Oak," said Michelle. "Oh, no!" She looked

embarrassed. "I can't remember the phone number."

"No problem," said Miss Gregg. "I'll get it next week."

So Michelle really couldn't remember it! She wasn't just putting me on. She had taken to school like a duck to water. After a few days of being called "the new girl," kids started calling her Michelle. The boys admired her from afar, and the girls invited her to eat lunch with them.

She was a good student, did her homework, and even though I fully expected her to show off—especially in social studies—she didn't.

"Do you have prayer requests today?" Miss Gregg looked at us.

"My grandfather is going into the hospital tomorrow," said Lisa. "He might need an operation."

"Who would like to pray for Lisa's grandfather?"

Kathy raised her hand. "Please, Jesus, help Lisa's grandfather. Help him not to be scared. Be with the doctors so they'll know what to do for him. And help Lisa and her family to have peace because they trust You. Amen."

"Thank you, Kathy. Someone else?" Miss Gregg asked.

Michelle raised her hand. "I'd like to thank the Lord for bringing us here."

Miss Gregg nodded.

"Thank you, Lord, for our safe trip. Bless my friends in California. Help Mom make new friends." I thought she was done, so I opened my eyes. Wrong! I closed them again. "And please, Lord, can we stay here a little longer? Amen." I guess amen is the clue that signals the end. Right?

"Someone else?" Miss Gregg waited. I suddenly felt very uncomfortable. "OK," she said, "let's talk about our lesson. What special event were Jesus and the disciples celebrating?"

"The Passover," I said. "They were remembering how God helped the Israelites get out of Egypt." That is one of my favorite stories. I even saw it on TV!

"That's right, Jennifer," said Miss Gregg. "Then why is it called the last supper?"

"Because it was their last time to be together before Jesus died," said Lisa.

"And Jesus told His friends something new," said Miss Gregg. "Who can tell us what it was?"

Michelle's hand shot up. "He said the bread represented His body and the cup represented His blood, and that He was going to die so people everywhere could be forgiven of their sins." It was in verse 27.

"In other words," Miss Gregg added, "Jesus was telling them His death would have a purpose. He would be dying for all of us."

"Why?" I asked.

"Because everyone needs a Savior," Laurie said. All the other girls nodded. I felt out of it. This was new to me.

"What do we call it now when we remember Jesus this way?" Miss Gregg asked.

"The Lord's Supper," said Kathy.

"Communion," said Lisa.

Well, how about that, Lord! I've always wondered what Communion was.

"You mean," I asked, "this was really the very first Communion?"

"That's right," Miss Gregg said. "And we keep celebrating it to help us remember Jesus until He comes back."

"Where do we do this?" I wondered. I didn't care if I looked stupid.

"In church," said Miss Gregg.

"I can see that I'm missing out on something by just going to Sunday school," I said.

Everyone smiled at me. I am finally catching on!

I hadn't even heard the bell. The boys were already in the car, and Mom was waiting for me. "Sorry," I said. "It was very important."

24

Who Will Run the Store?

Lord, it's me, Jennifer.

Talk about ups and downs! This is the first year since Grandma and Grandpa Green retired to Florida that we aren't going down for spring break. I am very disappointed. And so is everybody else.

Spring vacation is the highlight of the year. Grandma and Grandpa have a modern condominium with two bathrooms and a dishwasher. It even has new furniture. Grandma Green said her "northern" stuff would look out of place down there, because everyone else has white or bamboo. And besides, what was the use of owning a furniture store if you couldn't get new furniture when you wanted it? Finally Grandpa Green saw her point.

Well, the balcony has a view of the bluest water I've ever seen. And we can go swimming in the Gulf or a swimming pool. And we get to go fishing, which the boys love. Fishing is Pete's best sport! Grandma cooks anything we want or else we eat out.

"Your folks will be disappointed," Mom said to Dad. He had just announced that we weren't going.

"Well, we'll all be disappointed," Dad admitted. "But I just can't get away that week. I have meetings on the East coast the whole time."

"I don't think it's fair!" I said. "Just because of your dumb old meetings, we have to suffer."

"Enough of that, Jennifer," Dad said. "Someday you may understand what suffering really is. This is disappointing, yes, but, suffering, no."

"Some vacation for me," Mom said. "Three kids home with nothing to do and you off having a great time playing golf!"

"I will not be playing golf as you put it," Dad said. "I have important meetings."

"You always take your golf clubs," Pete observed. Dad ignored him.

"These meetings may affect us more than you know. You'll just have to take my word for it!"

Maybe this wasn't suffering, Lord, but it was as close to rebellion as I've ever seen our family.

"Hey, everybody," Dad said. "I'm sorry. I really am. But I just can't help it."

Mom took a deep breath. "We know, Dear." Then she

looked at us. "Grandma Andrews always says, 'If life gives you a lemon, make lemonade!'"

It sounded like Grandma Andrews all right.

"What's lemonade got to do with it?" Justin said. He isn't very good at analogies yet.

"Nothing," said Mom. "The point is we don't have to waste the week. Each of you think of something special you can do with a whole week's vacation. We'll talk about it later."

"Thanks, Sue," said Dad. He smiled at Mom. "Have I told you lately that I love you?"

The boys had already considered themselves dismissed. I guess I should have realized it, too. Our family has never been big on self-pity.

Upstairs in my room I picked up a pile of dirty clothes next to the bed. What could I do with a week's vacation? I could get my hair cut. Maybe I could learn to sew. My life was starting to look up.

At supper, Dad's grin clued us in that something was really up. "Mom's got an idea," he said. "Since we can't go to Florida, can you think of somebody else who'd enjoy going?"

We thought.

"Sarah and Michael!" I guessed. "They've only been down once. And it's their grandparents, too!" I could tell from Dad's reaction that I was right.

"Aunt Carol's spring vacation is the same as ours," Mom smiled. "I just checked." Aunt Carol teaches in another school district.

"Oh, they'd have such a good time," Pete said.

"But somebody has to take care of the store," I said. "They can't just close it. And Ruth always takes that week off." She's a salesperson.

"How about us?" Mom asked. "If everybody helped, do you think we could do it?" She paused. "Would you be willing to try?"

Dad looked serious. "I think Mom has a great idea. However, since I won't be here, she'll need all of you to help."

I tried to picture Mom helping customers choose furniture. Yes, she'd do OK. Could I help? I'm not really old enough, but I have experience. My bedroom is turning out great!

"I could help unload stuff," Pete said. He was getting excited. "I've watched Uncle Bob. I'm strong." Dad tried not to smile.

"What could I do?" asked Justin.

"You could be in charge of maintenance," Mom said. "Vacuuming, turning on lights, helping lock up. There'd be lots to do." Mom's face changed. "But how about deliveries?"

"Now that's a problem. But maybe they could wait for one week," Dad said. "Do you think you'd still have time to fit in your other plans for the week?"

"I couldn't think of anything special anyhow," Pete admitted.

"Me either," said Justin. "Could I have time off for Little League practice?"

"I think we could arrange that," Mom smiled. "Let's call Uncle Bob!"

"No," Dad said. "This is a big commitment. I want everybody to think it through first. We'll decide tomorrow night."

I considered my list. A haircut would only take an hour. I'd probably get time in the evenings to see my friends. And I could learn to sew during the summer. Besides, our cousins would have so much fun.

Well, we voted to try out storekeeping, and Dad chose himself to call his brother. "You have just won an all-expenses-paid vacation in beautiful, sunny Florida," Dad said, laughing. "No, don't hang up! It's Peter. Got an offer you can't refuse! Sue and the kids want to take care of the store so your family can spend spring break with Mom and Dad."

Dad listened. "No, we can't go anyway. I have a big business meeting on the east coast."

Dad listened, then laughed again. "I agree. And, after all, what can go wrong in a week?"

"Oh, I realize that," Dad replied. "I was only kidding. You know me! Yes. Well, talk it over and call us back. Right!"

We all watched Dad hang up the phone.

"Well?"

"I think he's overwhelmed. But I know he'd like to see Grandma and Grandpa. Can't you just picture him and Michael catching fish!" Dad's grin was exploding. The fizz was back in the ginger ale.

"And Sarah with a suntan!" I added.

"And Carol having some time to relax!" said Mom.

We waited twenty-three minutes until they called back. Even though Dad answered, we were all able to hear the excitement on the other end of the line.

"This is almost more fun than going ourselves." I said, and honestly meant it.

"I'd say you've squeezed a lemon into some super lemonade!" Dad announced.

Grandma Andrews couldn't have said it better!

"I still don't get it," said Justin.

Everybody laughed.

25

Spring Break

Lord, It's me, Jennifer.

Probably the hardest part of running the store was getting there in the morning. The boys were harder to get up than on school days. Mom tried to explain that it was the same kind of *responsibility,* but they had a harder time seeing her point. Especially with Dad gone.

Also, Mom isn't used to dashing off in the morning. And she didn't want to come home to a mess at night. So that meant loading the dishwasher, making the beds, and picking up.

Green's Furniture is one of the nicest around here. At least that's what a lot of people say. Some come from other towns to shop there.

The first day went smoothly. Mondays must be an off day for furniture buying. Mom waited on the few customers who came, but most were just looking. I opened the mail and sorted it into bills and checks and advertisements. Because Justin had Little League in the afternoon, he dusted and vacuumed in the morning. He isn't good at either one, as I'm sure You noticed right away.

There was one stock delivery, so Pete got to unpack some mirrors from North Carolina. By closing time, Mom was so tired she asked if we'd like to eat out. We went to Joe's Pizza. Guess who picked?

On Tuesday Michelle and her mother came in!

"Hi, Michelle!" I said. I was glad to see her.

"Hi! Do you work here?" she asked.

"Not really," I admitted, "it's my Uncle Bob's store. It used to belong to my grandparents, but they're retired in Florida now."

"Who's in Flordia?" she asked. She seemed confused.

"Well," I tried to explain, "actually everyone's in Florida. Uncle Bob's family is visiting Grandma and Grandpa Green in Florida for spring break. Mom and I are helping in the store while they're gone.

Just then Mom appeared wearing her brightest smile. "May I help you with something?" she asked.

"Mom," I said, "this is my friend, Michelle Stacy."

"And this is my mom," Michelle said.

Mrs. Stacy smiled just like Michelle. "Hi! I'm Kay Stacy. We've just moved here from California. I'm trying desperately to fit everything I had in the last house into the one here and it's very different. May we look around? I'll be needing a few things to fill in."

"Oh," said Mom, "I'm Sue Green. I'm just helping out in the store this week, but I'll be happy to answer any questions if I can."

"Thanks so much," said Mrs. Stacy. She and Michelle started off toward the bedroom furniture. I wondered if we should follow. Mom silently shook her head "no."

We tried to look busy. Mom straightened the drapery samples. I fluffed some couch cushions and rearranged the decorative pillows.

They spent about an hour in the store, looking at everything. "Such good taste!" Mrs. Stacy said.

"Thank you," Mom answered. "I can't take the credit, but I like it, too."

"You may think I'm silly," said Mrs. Stacy. "But I think there was a Bob Green in my husband's dorm in college." She mentioned the school.

"It's probably my brother-in-law," Mom said. "He and Carol met there."

"I can't believe it!" said Mrs. Stacy. "Talk about small worlds! Was her name Carol Carlson?"

I couldn't believe it either. At a small college does everybody know everyone else?

"Well," continued Mrs. Stacy, "I'll be back. I need some measurements. We'll be sure to call Bob and Carol when they get home."

"It was very nice to meet you," Mom said. "Thanks for stopping in."

"Bye, Jennifer," said Michelle.

"Bye. See you." After the door closed, I said, "Mom, did you notice her hair?"

"Yes, it's lovely."

"I mean Michelle's."

"Oh, hers was nice, too."

"It's the way I think I'd like mine. Do you think my neck is too long for that style?" I hoped not.

"Let's call Judy," Mom said. "Maybe she can work you in this week."

Well, I couldn't believe my good luck. I got an appointment at 3:30 that afternoon!

My hair's been growing since fifth grade, so naturally it was pretty long.

"Are you sure you want me to take off that much all at once?" Judy asked.

"Does it cost more?"

"No," Judy laughed. "It's just that it will be quite a dramatic change. Can you handle it?"

"Sure," I said. And if I couldn't, I'd never tell her! She sectioned it off into damp straggly sections. Then I couldn't see what she was doing, because my chair was facing away from the mirror. I watched a woman getting a permanent. When Judy swung me around, I nearly lost my breath.

"Wow!" I said.

"Hope you like it!"

"It sure is different. Do you think I look good this way?"

"Very 'in,'" said Judy. "It's the latest from California."

I wasn't surprised. What did surprise me was the way my hair sort of waved. It's always been straight as a board. "Where did the curl come from?"

"Partly the way it's cut," she answered. "And don't forget, you won't have all that weight dragging it down! I'll show you how to blow it dry."

I felt like two left feet. I was glad there weren't many people in the shop. "Will I ever catch on?"

"Sure," said Judy. "Everybody feels like that at first. It just takes practice."

I wouldn't have believed how much difference a haircut can make! I feel like a different Jennifer, at least on the outside.

Can You still tell it's me, Lord?

26

Invitation

Lord, it's the "new" Jennifer!

On Wednesday Laurie came in the store to see me. "Love your hair!" she said. "Who did it?"

"Judy."

"She's good!"

"Thanks."

Just then a customer went over to Mom to ask her advice on a drapery fabric. I hoped Mom wasn't in over her head, but she seemed comfortable as she spoke with the woman.

"Thinking of changing careers?" Laurie asked.

"Well," I said, "I don't think so, but this is fun."

"What are you wearing to Michelle's party?"

My heart stopped beating. "Party?"

"Friday night." Then she realized she had blown it.

"Oh, Jennifer, I'm sorry! I really am. I was sure she'd asked you."

"Oh, don't worry about it," I said quickly. "I couldn't go anyway. The store is always open Friday nights. In fact, that's one of our busiest times. Mom certainly couldn't handle it alone!"

"Right," agreed Laurie. "I just love your hair."

"You said that before."

"Well, I really do," Laurie said. "It's absolutely beautiful. Hey, I have to go. Can you come over tomorrow night?"

"I have other plans." It was a lie.

"Well, see ya."

"Uh huh." I watched her leave. I think it's the first time since kindergarten I've been left out. I had to bite my tongue so I wouldn't cry.

Mom finished recommending an eggshell casement fabric. "Laurie gone already? Something wrong?"

"I don't want to talk about it."

"Sometimes it helps," Mom said.

"No." I still couldn't believe it.

"Well," said Mom slowly, "if you feel like telling me, let me know."

Just then a delivery man came in. "I have an order," he said. Mom signed for it and called Pete.

"Want me to uncrate it?" Pete asked.

"If you can do it without damaging anything."

"I'll be careful, Mom." Pete disappeared into the warehouse area. I followed him, mainly to get away from Mom.

"Looks like a bed," Pete said. "Maybe it's yours."

"Oh, sure," I pouted. The funny thing was he was right.

"Mom," I said, "it's beautiful!"

"It certainly is," she agreed as we went back into the store. She's developing a good sense of knowing when to back off. She didn't say anything else.

Suddenly I was sobbing. "She doesn't want me . . . And I was so nice . . . And now she's taking away all my friends . . . It's all Dad's fault . . . Why does he have to be a sales engineer? . . . It's just because her father is a dumb Christian leader . . . I thought we were supposed to love each other like Jesus."

Mom just let me ramble. Finally I quit crying and took the tissue she handed me.

"Life give you another lemon?" Mom asked.

"I guess so," I sniffed. "Being left out sure feels awful!"

"Is there someone outside your group you could call for Friday night?"

"Not Harriet Peats!"

"Well, I didn't have anybody in particular in mind," she said. "Why don't you sleep on it?"

I grinned. "Grandma Andrews?"

Mom nodded and smiled back.

We ate out again. I was beginning to wonder if mothers

who had careers ever cooked any meals at all for their families.

On the way into the house, Mom picked up the mail. "Hey," she said, "here's something for you, Jennifer."

"For me?" It was the size of a birthday card. No return address. I opened it in the kitchen and read it silently.

"Mom," I said, "listen to this!

> *Dear Jennifer,*
>
> *I'm having a few girls over Friday night at 7:30 for supper (very informal—that means jeans!). Hope you can come! I mailed this because I especially wanted you to know how much I appreciated your friendliness my first day of school. If it hadn't been for you, I don't think I could have made it! Thank you very much!!!!!*
>
> *Love, from your new friend,*
>
> *Michelle"*

"That's lovely, isn't it?" Mom said.

"I can go, can't I?"

"Well," Mom smiled. "I think Green's Furniture can manage without you one more Friday night!"

27

Homecoming

Lord, it's Jennifer again.

Suddenly the week was over and Green's Furniture was still alive. In fact, we had sold a blue sofa, a gold chair, a kitchen table-and-chair set, a brass table lamp, and taken an order for custom draperies for a living and dining room.

Just as we were closing on Saturday, Dad walked in.

"How was the lemonade stand?" he laughed.

"Hey, Dad!" The boys shoved each other out of the way to get to him. "Welcome home!"

Mom's turn was next. She got a big hug and an extra big grin. "You know," he said, "you are something else! I'm so proud of you! Everything go OK?"

"Great!" Mom hugged him back. "We missed you, though. How was your week? Time for golf?"

"Nope! But I'll tell you all about it later."

My turn. "Well, what have we here?" Dad asked. I hoped he'd like my hair. His approval means a lot to me, as You know.

"Fantastic! Let's see the back."

I turned around slowly.

"A beautiful young lady!" He grinned. "However, I must have forgotten to tell you that you are not allowed to grow up!" He pretended to be serious but his eyes were smiling.

"Dad!" I laughed.

"Now, for a special treat, we're all going out for dinner!" Dad announced. "Your mother deserves a chance to get out of that kitchen." I looked at Pete and Justin, but nobody told. Mom's secret was safe!

Sunday was Easter so I got to go to both Sunday school and church, as I'm sure You noticed. Do You have an attendance book?

In Sunday school we read in the Bible where it says that Jesus really did come alive again. It's called *resurrection*. Miss Gregg said this is very important because it makes Jesus special. He's different from leaders of other religions. We sang a song called "He Lives." Everybody must like it because they sang loud.

At church time we met Mom and Dad, and we sat together as a family like we did for Christmas. I felt wonderful. This time I glanced around during the anthem and saw several kids in my class sitting with their families. Michelle's father looks just like any other man. Can You see something different in him, Lord?

In the afternoon we met the plane from Florida. I could just tell that everybody had a good time. Even Uncle Bob got a tan.

"You'll never know what this meant to us!" Uncle Bob hugged Mom. "Everything go OK? You didn't call once. I even managed to forget we have a store!"

"No problems," Mom said, smiling. "I really enjoyed it. Maybe I'll ask for a job."

Well, everyone was talking at once. There was a lot to catch up on. I told Sarah about Michelle's party. As You know, the best I've ever gone to!

Looking back on it, Lord, I guess I never realized how great it makes you feel to do something special for someone else. Good grief! Now *I'm* beginning to sound like Grandma Andrews!

28

Mom's Date

Dear Lord, it's me, Jennifer.

Mom seems more like a person than she used to. Today I got a glimpse of a young girl locked up inside her, trying to get out. She acted almost silly when Dad came home from work early.

He said, "Come on, Sue. We're going out for a cup of coffee."

"But, Peter, I'm right in the middle of fixing dinner. And the children . . ." Her voice trailed off.

"It'll wait." He just stood there grinning. I love it when my dad grins.

Naturally Mom took her apron off and put on fresh lipstick. I mean, what else could she do? It isn't as if Dad comes home early every day. In fact, lately he hardly comes home at all.

I didn't even mind when Mom said, "Jennifer, will you fix salads and finish the pudding? And take out the casserole at 6:10 if we aren't back?" I was tempted to pout a little on general principles, but it wasn't worth the effort. They were out the door anyway.

To be honest, I really don't think about my parents a lot. I spend most of my time thinking about myself.

I was thinking about Arnold Pelikan while I stirred the pudding. He never did follow up on that note! Suddenly the door banged open and Justin flew into the kitchen with Pete two steps behind. Pete was yelling, "You creep! Now you've done it for the last time!"

"Hey, close the door," I called, but by now they were halfway up the stairs. I could hear that Justin had been caught. Personally, I didn't know whether to go after them, close the door, or keep stirring the pudding. I began to realize what mothers are up against. I closed the door on my way upstairs. By now they were hollering and pounding on each other right in the middle of the stairway.

"Stop it!" I shouted. But they didn't even hear me. Clearly there was no way I could establish my own authority when they couldn't care less if I was even there. Feeling totally helpless, I returned to the kitchen.

Just in time, I might add. The pudding was beginning to burn on the bottom of the pan, so I tried to stir it only on top before pouring the good part into five small dishes. Then I realized it was 6:10 because the timer on the stove began to blast off. I was so busy trying to turn off the buzzer, and so relieved when the noise stopped, that I forgot to take the casserole out of the oven.

I still hadn't started the salads. "Easy does it," I said, trying to keep calm. I quickly cut up some lettuce, added some little tomatoes, and stuck two different bottles of dressing next to the salt and pepper.

"Oh, no, the casserole," I gasped, as the oven began to smoke. I rescued it almost in time.

My brothers were now so quiet, I was really worried. As I headed for the stairs, Mom and Dad walked in, still smiling, sort of like Linda Cummings and Bruce Jones after math.

"Well, Jennifer," Dad said, "I see you have everything under control. Thanks for my coffee date with your mom."

"Dinner's ready, more or less," I told them. "But the boys had an awful fight and now they've disappeared."

"Par for the course," said Mom, as she headed for the kitchen. "Is something burning?"

"Pete, Justin, come down here at once," Dad called. I could hear their bedroom door opening and both boys talking at once.

"You're grounded for tomorrow! And get right down here for dinner. No excuses," Dad added.

Suddenly I realized I hadn't thought of myself once in the past hour. I really hadn't had time!

29

Dad's Surprise

Dear Lord, it's me, Jennifer.

Have You heard the news? We're moving to Philadelphia!

Dad got the news yesterday, and he wanted to tell Mom first. He got a big promotion. He's going to be Vice President of Sales on the East coast which means he'll be in charge!

"It's really an honor!" Dad said. He was trying not to brag but he wanted us to know that it's a big step up. His grin had become more of a glow.

"When will we move?" Justin asked.

"Right after school's out. Since it's so close to the end, Mom and I want you to finish the school year here. I'll probably spend most of my time on the East coast from now on, but I'll be home every weekend."

Mom nodded. "Of course, we'll have to sell this house and buy a new one there. You'll each be able to have your own room." She looked at the boys.

Suddenly I thought of my own room. "Just when I got it all fixed up!"

"You can take your furniture along, Jennifer. And I'm sure we can get the same wallpaper in Philadelphia if you still want it," Mom explained.

"Of course I want it," I said.

"One of the best things is that I'll be home more," Dad explained. "I won't have to keep going East, because I'll already be there."

"Is that why you were gone so much?" Pete wanted to know.

"Well, that's part of it," Dad said. "Hey, I've missed all of you a lot!"

"We've missed you, too, Dad," I said. "Congratulations!" I went over and hugged him.

"I'm glad your company realizes how *responsible* you are!" Mom added. "You've certainly earned this!" She was happy for Dad and proud of him. Could You tell?

"Where is Philadelphia?" Justin asked. He has trouble finding his way out of a closet. And, to be honest, I know more about Switzerland than I do about the United States.

"Finish your milk," Mom reminded. "And then we'll get out the encyclopedia."

"Here," said Dad, as he pointed to a map of the United States, "here is Illinois where we live now. And over here is Pennsylvania. Philadelphia is on the side nearest the ocean."

"Where do they make the pencils?" Justin wanted to know.

Everyone except Pete looked blank. "Not pencils, Dummy, Pennsylvania."

"That's what I said," defended Justin.

"Hold on, guys," Dad said. "Sylvania means woods. It's a beautiful state with lots of hills and trees."

"What a change!" said Mom. "I've always wanted to live in a place with hills and trees! What an adventure!"

"Can I take my rock collection along?" Pete wondered.

"You bet you can," Dad said. "Everything we own will be packed in a big moving van and delivered to our new house."

"What new house?" asked Justin.

"The one we'll be buying," Mom said again. "We'll sell this one and buy another home there." I've never seen Mom so excited.

"What's the climate like?" I asked. "Will we still have snow?" As You know, I've learned about climate in social studies.

"Not too different from here. But the winters usually aren't as long or as cold. Sometimes there's plenty of snow. The springs and falls are beautiful." Dad sounded like a used car salesman on TV.

I sure didn't want to be the only killjoy, but all of a sudden I remembered Sarah. "But we can't take our family with us!" I blurted out.

"No," Dad agreed. "But we can come back to see them, and they can come to visit us. Like we do with Grandpa and Grandma Green. We'll get a big house so we can have lots of company."

Well, Lord, going to bed is hard. I'm all mixed up. This is the only home I've ever lived in, the only room I've ever had. But ahead of us lies adventure, excitement, the unknown. Lord, I feel pulled in both directions at once! Do You understand how I feel?

30

Another Surprise

Lord, it's your friend, Jennifer.

Are You ever surprised? In other words, have You known about our move for a long time?

Last night was sort of a wide-awake dream. Dad's announcement, I mean. The sort of thing that happens to somebody else. That's probably because we've been so permanent. I mean, when even your grandparents live in your town, how much more permanent can things get?

Today at school I still felt mixed up. I didn't want to brag about Dad. And I don't want my friends to think that I'm excited about leaving them, because I'm not. So I did the only thing I know how to do—I was honest.

"When will you be going?" Laurie wanted to know.

"Not till school's out. So there's a while yet."

"I'll have a party for you," she said, "on one condition."

"What's that?" I asked.

"You've got to promise to write and tell me all about everything. I want to be your friend always—even when we're old and in college."

"Of course I'll write. I'd do that anyway," I assured her. "And you've got to promise you'll come to visit me just as soon as you can."

"That would be a ball!" she said. Laurie's like me—never been anywhere. "Will you come back to see us?"

"Sure," I said. "Don't forget half our family still lives here."

"Hey, that's right!"

By then we were outside the math room.

Well, every time I told somebody else, the move seemed more real. And at supper that's all my family talked about. Mom said her parents are not too thrilled. Besides Mom and Aunt Mary, they have Uncle David, but he lives in Missouri.

Back in my room, I still felt a little sad. That's when I remembered my birthday cards. I took down the one from Sarah and read it again. It was about God's love and care.

Lord, You *are* my special friend! And I can still keep telling You everything, even in Pennsylvania! I assume You're coming along! Do You have any friends there already? Are there any churches in Pennsylvania?

Suddenly I saw my problem. I ran down to see Dad. He was alone in the living room.

"Dad," I said, "something's bothering me."

"Sit down, Jennifer. Let's talk."

I sat on the ottoman. "Dad, whenever you mentioned spending time in 'the East,' I always pictured you in some kind of office. The East has never seemed like a real place where people live."

"I'm not sure I understand, Jennifer."

"What I mean is, does it have houses and neighborhoods and grocery stores and schools. And churches?"

Dad began to smile. "I do see what you mean!"

"Now that I really think about it," I said slowly, "people must live there just like people live in Switzerland."

"You're right, Jennifer, and I've got an idea. What if sometime soon we all fly out for a weekend so everyone can see what it's like? We'll need to start looking for a house anyway."

"Oh, Dad, can we?"

"The more I think about it, the better I like the idea. Mom and I will start making some plans. Then you can see for yourself that there really are houses and stores and even historical places."

"Dad, I love you!"

"I love you, too!" And then he got that I've-got-a-secret look. "There's something else there that might interest you!"

I tried to guess, but all I could think of was boys! I didn't want to say that, so I laughed and said, "I give up."

"What would you say if I told you there are horses?"

"*Horses!*" I couldn't believe it! I was more excited than I had ever been in my whole life!

"You can start riding lessons right after we get settled."

Well, I hugged him and squealed like a two-year-old. Dad seemed as excited as I was. But then he got a phone call so I came back to my room.

Well, Lord, You heard it first!

As a matter of fact, I wonder if You'll have to keep me from falling off!

How lucky can some kids get?

It seems like Eric and Alison, the Thorne twins, are always running into adventure. The most ordinary things become unusual when they are involved.

The Great UFO Chase   In this seventeenth book of the series, a brainy student visits the Thornes, and brings with him a lot more than his books! Is it purely coincidental that residents of Ivy, Illinois, begin sighting UFO's just after this stranger arrives? What kind of transmission is disturbing the radio-station signals, and why are Air Force officials interested in the Thornes' houseguest? Eric asks these questions and more before he finally finds the answers to *The Great UFO Chase*.

The Olympic Plot   Alison unknowingly becomes a threat to the lives of the President and Vice President of the United States. She knows only that she is not in complete control of her actions, and that she forgets segments of time. How can she help Eric uncover the plot when neither of them is sure there *is* a plot? Their visit to Olympic Village becomes a nightmare of kidnappings, fake athletes, and sickness, while the time for murder draws closer and closer.

Secret of Pirates' Cave   When a classmate of Eric's presents an exciting report of how pirates once raided his ancestors, Eric repeats the story at home. He and Alison are thrilled to discover that their own ancestors were on the same ship, and were raided by the same pirate. Mr. Thorne shows them half of a map that supposedly leads to the families' treasure, and the search is on!

Before the treasure can be recovered, the kids must deal with secret tunnels, a "monster cave," and a ghost who doesn't want the past disturbed!

If you like adventure stories, be sure to read these and other books in the Thorne Twin series.